have created. They don't know what to do with her once they've got her. Being no-hopers makes them more dangerous to deal with, not less..." Like many of Martin's stories (some written under the pseudonym Catherine Sefton), the book is set in Northern Ireland, where he lives. Among his other books for older children are *The Life and Loves of Zoë T. Curley*, *Tango's Baby* and the Irish trilogy *Beat of the Drum*, *Frankie's Story* and *Starry Night*, which won the Other Award.

Martin Waddell writes books for a wide range of ages. He has twice won the Smarties Book Prize – for *Farmer Duck* and *Can't You Sleep, Little Bear?* – as well as the Kurt Maschler Award and the Best Books for Babies Award. His other books include *The Haunting of Ellen*, *In a Blue Velvet Dress*, *The Ghost and Bertie Boggin*, *Cup Final Kid*, *The Perils of Lord Reggie Parrot*, *The Dump Gang*, *My Aunty Sal and the Mega-sized Moose*, *Fred the Angel*, *Little Obie and the Kidnap* and *Little Obie and the Flood*.

Books by the same author

Beat of the Drum

Frankie's Story

Starry Night

The Haunting of Ellen

In a Blue Velvet Dress

Tango's Baby

The Life and Loves of Zoë T Curley

THE KIDNAPPING OF SUZIE Q

MARTIN WADDELL

WALKER BOOKS
AND SUBSIDIARIES
LONDON · BOSTON · SYDNEY

First published 1994 by Hamish Hamilton
under the name of Catherine Sefton

This edition published 2000 by Walker Books Ltd
87 Vauxhall Walk, London SE11 5HJ

2 4 6 8 10 9 7 5 3 1

This book has been typeset in Sabon.

Printed in Great Britain by Cox & Wyman Ltd
Reading, Berkshire

British Library Cataloguing in Publication Data
A catalogue record for this book is
available from the British Library.

ISBN 0-7445-6989-3

For Sarah, who smiles a lot

CHAPTER ONE

I blame The Limp Boyle's old goats.

If it hadn't been for them, we would have been in and out of Semple's Supermarket before the robbery happened, and safely on our way to pick up Ruth from the Long Route bus. But the goats got in the way and I ended up half dead on Stonecutters Mountain.

"Quick in, get the things, and quick out again, Suzie!" Mum said, as we ran across the car park behind Semple's Supermarket. And that is when The Limp's wife, Mrs Teresa Boyle, penned us in with her shopping trolley.

"Mrs Quinn! Mrs Quinn!" panted Mrs Boyle. "Just one word, Mrs Quinn, dear. I'll not hold you up, for I can see you are in a hurry, but The Limp is very upset."

"I'm in a terrible hurry, Teresa," Mum said. "Ruth's coming off the bus from Belfast and I have to meet her at the crossroads."

"I'll not hold you a minute!" Teresa said, grabbing Mum's arm to keep her anchored, and then she launched into her story.

The Limp Boyle is the Cloughanny Goat Man. The Limp tethers his goats out on the coast road, and one of the new people in the big bungalows along there had been making a fuss. It seems this new one had it in her head that The Limp's goats were a traffic hazard. She'd been into the police and on to the Roads Department about them, and The Limp was hopping mad and threatening to tether his goats in her garden, to eat all her fancy garden centre plants.

"Maybe you'd sort it out for us, Mrs Quinn," Teresa asked plaintively.

"Well, I'll see what I can do, Teresa," Mum said, looking at her watch. "Now, if you really don't mind, I must be... "

Teresa really did mind, and she told us so. Part of her was annoyed on behalf of the goats, and the other part was heart-scared of what The Limp might do. The Limp has earned a bad name around Cloughanny. He has a drink problem.

Mum put on her Elected Local Councillor hat and spent a solid five minutes calming her down, which meant that it was 4:35 when we walked into Semple's.

Despite anything the police say, we *know* that the robbery took place eight minutes later, at 4:43 exactly, by which time I was second in

8

the queue and Mum had just left me to go back for birthday candles she had missed. Getting the stuff for my little brother Davie's birthday was the whole purpose of the shopping. We'd dumped Davie on Mrs Flynn down the lane so he wouldn't see the stuff until the party.

"Hold on to the trolley," she said. "And don't go dreamy on me and lose your place in the queue." Then she added, "No slipping any of your little extras into the trolley, Suzie Q!" and gave me a smile.

Mum meant chocolate. I have a thing about chocolate, and Mum has a thing about my waistline, but the waistline is on me, and not her, and anyway, she is not one to be talking.

"Would I?" I said, all innocent.

"You would!" she said, and she bounced off up the aisle.

Mum didn't know it, but the extra chocolate was already in the trolley, carefully hidden beneath the buns. Not only chocolate either – I'd slipped myself some cheese and onion crisps as well. The crisps were for when we got back to the car. I was promising myself a crisps feast to build up my strength for Davie's party, and the chocolate was my compensation for having to help with the shopping.

Then Danny Semple came out of his office and walked slowly towards the till. There were two big lumps of boys with him. They were in cheap anoraks, with the hoods up, and they had scarves over their faces. One of them might have been seventeen or eighteen; the other might have been a bit older. They were wearing identical scruffy trainers and jeans.

Danny came up to May at the checkout and said, "Open your till, May."

The way he said it made me look up.

Oh God, no! I thought.

If I'd kept cool, abandoned the trolley and gone up the aisle after Mum, I would have been all right, but I didn't, because I was second in the queue and Mum had told me not to lose my place. It was plain daft of me, but there it is.

"I'm busy with this lady, Daddy," May said, batting for the Customer Courtesy of the Month Award. She was in mid-checkout on Mrs Doherty's dog food, skipping the cans over the scanner and flipping her buttons.

"Open it now, May," Danny said. "These *gentlemen* have come to take our money."

Then everything happened at once.

There was an old countryman last in the line, very much *not* the kind of man you would expect to do what he did. I don't know him to talk to, but his name is Bertie-something and he has a few stony fields along Mountain Road. I have seen him riding down into Cloughanny and pedalling his bike back home up the hill.

He stepped out of the line. He had one hand gripping his basket, and in the other he was holding a can of baked beans, the big size. He still had his bicycle clips on.

The next thing I knew, the man had chucked the beans can. It smashed into the older boy's face. He went reeling back from the force of the can hitting him, and the old man followed up by tackling the other one. The two of them went over in a bundle at my feet.

They were rolling around struggling on the floor. The first one got back on his feet and started kicking at the man, knocking him backwards against my trolley. The trolley skewed around, forcing me against the counter, and effectively cutting off my prospects of retreat.

The bigger boy grabbed me from behind as I tried to move clear of the trolley trap.

His hand went over my mouth and he grabbed my arm, pulled it behind my back, and twisted it up. He pulled my head back against his shoulder. All the witnesses who saw it say he had a gun held to my head, but if he had, I didn't see it. If he had one hand on my mouth and one hand twisting my arm up behind my back, I don't see how he could have had a gun, unless he held it in his teeth … but there you go, that is what the witnesses say. I know Leo – his name was Leo – had a gun, but I don't see how he can have used it during the robbery. Maybe I am wrong. It was all so quick and all so terrifying that I must have got it mixed up somehow.

"Nobody do anything or she gets it," he

11

shouted at the rest of the queue. Mrs Doherty put her hand over her mouth. The two behind me, a woman and a girl with a runny nose, stood there looking at each other. None of them seemed to take in what was happening. Nobody moved a muscle to help, which says a bit about the community spirit Mum is always talking about fostering. Old Bertie was lying on the floor groaning, but no one went to help him either.

"Grab the money!" Leo shouted.

"Give us the money, you!" Gerard yelled at May. Of course I didn't know he was called Gerard then, not that it would have made much difference if I had. He just yelled, but he didn't do anything about getting the money himself – which was typical of Gerard.

Poor May blinked at him in terror. Then she looked at her dad. Danny certainly wasn't going to risk his beer belly in a fight, so May was getting no assistance from that quarter.

Gerard reached past May and grabbed the money from the till, stuffing it in his anorak pocket. Most of it, that is. Some of the money went on the floor.

Then they made for the door, pulling me along with my shoes clattering on the tiled floor.

Nobody did anything to stop Leo and Gerard from taking me. It must have been about ten metres to the door and they were running me between them, but absolutely nobody else moved a muscle or spoke. The story now is that Leo was waving his gun about and threatening to shoot. As I say, I have my doubts about whether he had the gun out or not. I didn't see the gun then. I had that pleasure later.

We were now out in the open. They had a van waiting just behind the trolley rack, with the two back doors wide open and the driver revving the engine, just like a film on TV.

They were dragging me towards the van when I woke up and got my arm free. I made a grab at Leo, yelling, "Let me go! Let me go!" and tried to twist away from him.

My fingers caught his scarf and I half got it off over his nose.

He reacted instantly, slamming me around backwards so that I smashed the back of my head against the top of the door frame. I went down on the pavement, grappling at his knees. The next moment, he lifted me up on to my feet and toppled me over into the van.

I'm convinced that Leo and Gerard never meant to take me. It was sheer panic on their part. Nothing would have been easier than to leave me there on the Semples' forecourt, but they drove off with me flat on my face in the back of the van.

And that was just the beginning of my troubles!

CHAPTER TWO

You might ask: where was her mother when all that was going on?

She'd gone up the aisle for the candles, and Semple's store is L-shaped, with the office at the short end of the L, around the corner from the tills.

So Danny Semple and the two robbers, on their way out of Danny's office, brushed past Mum as she was reaching up for the birthday candles. She says Danny was staring straight in front of him, and she thought he looked popeyed and strange, and something clicked in her mind, just as it did in mine.

Danny was approaching the till, and Mum says she was going to shout a warning but then realized that that wasn't going to do any good.

Mum is quick on the uptake, quicker than I was anyway.

I froze, but she acted.

She turned around and went back to the office. She says she was half afraid there would be another one of them there, covering the telephone, but there wasn't.

She closed the office door behind her and locked it on the inside. Then she got the telephone down on the floor and crouched beneath the desk so that she would be out of sight and out of the way of any bullets that might be flying about. She dialled the police, to report a robbery in progress.

Mum is dead sure about when she telephoned, because there was an advertising clock on the wall above Danny Semple's desk and it said 4:43. Danny says that clock keeps good time, and Mum had no reason to make the time up. We were to meet Ruth at the Kilturn crossroads at five to five; the crossroads is about five minutes in the car from Cloughanny along the Ballydorn Road, and we were just bordering on being late, so 4:43 must be about right.

I think she was brilliant. I don't know how she kept her head, but she did.

She gave the cops a running commentary as the robbery was going on, although it didn't amount to much, because even my Wonder Mum can't see around corners.

She couldn't see, but she could hear, and what she heard was the commotion with the beans can followed by shouting and bumps.

15

She was busy praying that I hadn't done something stupid and become involved in trying to stop them, but she did what the policewoman on the other end of the telephone said: she stayed put and didn't move.

Mum is *absolutely* definite that it was a policewoman on the other end, not a man.

The next thing she heard was lots of shouting and somebody banging and rattling at the locked door, trying to open it.

"It's locked, Daddy!" she heard somebody say.

Then she knew it wasn't the robbers and she got herself out and unlocked the door.

Big May Semple was standing there crying. Danny Semple charged past her into the office, and there was a daft moment when he stood there staring at where his telephone should have been, not seeing that Mum had the receiver still clutched in her hand.

"What the hell are you doing in here?" Danny shouted at Mum.

"Talking to the police!" Mum said.

She was going to hand him the telephone but Danny grabbed it from her and started gabbling down the line that he'd been robbed, which the police knew already anyway.

"Where were yous? Where were yous?" Danny yelled down the phone at the police, which, considering that Ballydorn Police Station is a good fifteen-minute drive away, wasn't very smart of him.

Meanwhile, Mum had raced up towards the checkout looking for me. Of course she didn't find me.

"Them two lads took her in their van," Mrs Doherty told her.

Mum says her heart stopped, and then she went back to the office, hauling Danny off the telephone and yelling blue murder down the phone about her Suzie Q being kidnapped.

Much good it did her!

We know the robbery was at 4:43, because that is when it happened, but the first police car didn't show up until nearly a quarter past five, and what everybody wants to know is, where the police were in between times.

That's where the Police Station record doesn't square up with what we know happened.

They have it in Ballydorn that a Constable McCormick took the call, and he has it logged at 4:55, which gives them a response time of about twenty minutes from logging the call to arrival at the scene of the crime. Given the winding nature of the road from Ballydorn to Cloughanny, that would be fair enough, if it was true. We are way out in the wilds, and you can't expect to have a police car around every corner but, by our calculation, the real response time was nearer thirty-two minutes – from 4:43 to 5:15.

That is a long way of saying that if the police

in Ballydorn had responded more quickly, their police car might have reached the Kilturn crossroads and been heading down to Cloughanny *before* the van could make it to the main road. All they'd have had to do then was put their police car across the road, and it would have been like putting a cork in a bottle. The van, with me and the robbers in it, would have been trapped, with nowhere to go but up one of the farm lanes. Then, when more help arrived, it would have been easy enough to find it, because the place is so bare and barren that hiding a van full of people would be impossible.

I wish the police had been a bit quicker, but I suppose I can't really blame them. Here in Northern Ireland the police have problems. Together with the British Army, they are up against the IRA. The IRA wants a thirty-two county United Ireland, with the British out of the six counties that make up Northern Ireland – and they believe that that is a cause worth fighting and killing for. Most of the people they kill, when they are not leaving random bombs around the place, are policemen. One of the ways they do this is to get the police out on a fake call to some incident and then blow them to pieces. So, naturally enough, when the police get a panic call to send a car out to the middle of nowhere, they stop and think before they go. If the police made a mistake, it was to err on the side of caution, and I'd be cautious enough if I was a policeman, knowing there were gunmen out there waiting to get me.

When it comes to mistakes, it is my kidnappers you have to look at. The kidnapping was an accident, of course, the result of their panic, but the whole thing was a botch, really. No respectable thief would set off to rob a store in a small town that has only one road out of it, a road that winds this way and that between the rocks, with always the possibility of a herd of cows or sheep blocking the way, or getting caught behind a manure spreader or a tractor.

My three robbers, Leo and Gerard and Dodie (I haven't mentioned her before, but she was the one driving the van), did just that, which only goes to show that they were total incompetents, amateurs. That didn't make them a whole lot easier to deal with. It made them more dangerous, not less.

CHAPTER THREE

I have no idea what way the getaway van went, because I had two big lads wrestling with me and, before I knew where I was, they had a blanket over my head.

I tried thrashing about, but it was no good at all. They must have weighed about a ton between them. They got me pinned down and then they started yelling at each other.

"Get her out!" somebody shouted.

"Shut her up!"

I don't know who was doing the shouting. Probably most of it was Leo. He was the leader, and he gave the orders, and old softie Gerard did what he was told, but their panic had upset their usual arrangements, and Gerard was yelling back. It just shows how wired up they were.

I was choking and struggling, and they clamped my body against the back of the front seat and forced me down again. I remember realizing that there were three of them: the two who had been in the shop and another one who must have been waiting in the van. I knew that one of the voices belonged to a girl, but I am a dead loss on bumps on the road or anything that might have been helpful to the police later. Right then I wasn't much worried about the police anyway. I had problems of a more immediate nature to cope with, like: are these ones going to kill me?

That is the kind of problem which concentrates the mind wonderfully.

The van slithered. The one kneeling with his knee in my back started trying to open the door.

"You can't. You'll kill her!" somebody shouted.

"Chuck her out!"

"She's seen my face! She's seen my face!"

"That bloody doesn't matter!"

"It bloody does to me!"

"Get her out!"

"She knows me! She knows me!"

I started kicking, and then he pummelled me in the back and banged me down again.

"Don't hurt her!" came from Dodie. I remember wondering how a girl had got mixed up in it. With the panic I was in, it seems amazing that I had time to think that, but I did.

"Get her out!"

"She saw my face. She knows me. She bloody well knows who I am."

"Get her bloody out! What did you bloody get her in for? Are you crazy?"

"She saw my face!"

All this yelling and shouting was going on, and there I was, scared stiff and thinking I had to do something but not knowing what to do or how to start doing it, with about 12 stone lying across my back, banging my blanket-covered head on the floor of the van.

Of course I hadn't seen Leo's face at all. That pleasure was denied me until much later. I'd just clawed his scarf down over his nose. How could I recognize anybody in those circumstances?

I started struggling again for the umpteenth time, because the blanket was tight around my neck and I thought I'd be strangled or smothered, and then someone banged my head down again, shouting, "You stay still."

I know I ought to have kept on struggling, but I didn't.

Maybe they'll stop in a minute and dump me out of the van, I thought, but it didn't happen.

They kept yelling and cursing at each other, set on proving that they were the most stupid hold-up artists ever. They had managed to come out with what can't have been more than a few pounds from the till … and me. What would they do about me when they got me home?

I started crying, great big hysterical sobs that I couldn't stop. I have never been so frightened as I was in that van, knowing that they were terrified and out of control, and that there wasn't anything I could do to save myself.

I remember thinking, *If I get through this, I can get through anything.*

That is all I can remember about the van ride.

Maybe that isn't as silly as it sounds. I was flat out in the back of the van with a blanket over my head, unable to see anything, breathing blood from the nosebleed that had started when they slammed me against the back of the van, and being sat on.

I don't know whether the changeover from the van to the car was worked at Plumber's Point, or if they had the car waiting for them at the Woman's house. I think I would remember being lifted out of the van and into the back seat of a car, if it happened. But on the other hand, I was tied up and gagged with an old scarf at some stage, and I don't remember that happening either.

My impression is that we drove to the Woman's house and I was unloaded. Then I think Leo must have driven the van down to Plumber's Point, with Gerard following on his famous motorbike. When they'd set the van on fire, they would both have come back to the Woman's house on the bike. The police think it didn't happen that way; why, I don't know, as they didn't take me into their confidence.

The police theory at the time seems to have been that my three didn't do the dumping, and that there must have been a fourth person involved, probably the Woman. The fact that my memory of what happened to me doesn't fit their story they regard as a minor inconvenience. Their theory is that I blacked out when I was in the van, and was moved, unconscious, into the car, and that is why I don't remember it.

What nobody can argue about is that the van was found, half burnt out, at the tourist viewpoint above Plumber's Point five hours later – that would be just before ten. Some couple had gone up there for a quiet romantic session, and there was this van smouldering away in the light of their headlights. It was funny, because apparently the couple who found the van weren't supposed to be a couple, and they certainly weren't supposed to be all alone at Passenger's Lake gazing at the moon.

They must have faced a real dilemma. But they were good citizens, because the man drove down to the police station and reported what he'd found. The police were very coy about his identity, presumably because he had helped them.

Helped them find the getaway van, that is, not helped them find me. As it worked out, the police finding the van didn't help me one bit.

CHAPTER FOUR

My next clear memory is of being carried and Dodie talking to me.

"You're all right. You're all right. Shush now, you're all right," she kept saying. It was a small, soft voice, and I remember even then being comforted by it, despite everything, with a hazy kind of notion that because she was a girl she would defend me.

"Tell her if she doesn't shut up, she won't be!" Leo said.

"We're in enough trouble already," Dodie said.

"Who do you think the whole thing was in aid of, eh?"

"I never asked for this. I never wanted this!" came from Dodie.

"Well, you've got it now, Dodie," Leo said.

Dodie. It was the first name I managed to pick up, but it didn't mean anything to me.

"Only don't you dare hurt her any more. She looks like she's hurt bad enough as it is. All that blood! Would you look at my shoes?"

She must have had my blood on her shoes. Considering that the blood was seeping out of my nose, through the blanket, I can't say I had much sympathy for her.

Leo hadn't either. He called her a few names as they lugged me along.

"Are you all right?" she asked, close up to my muffled head.

More mumbles from me in the blanket. It is difficult to say much when you have a gag in your mouth.

"Nobody's going to hurt you, so shush now!"

If I'd been able to bawl her out, I would have. I was scared out of my wits, and telling me to shush now wasn't very helpful.

I thought they were going to dump me, and I wondered whether they would leave me all bound up in a ditch, or whether they would unwrap me from my blanket so I could walk. But it didn't work out that way.

I *think* I was taken into a barn of some sort at the Woman's house because there were agricultural smells; that is as far as I can go. I didn't hear any animal sounds, so I can't even be sure if I was on a farm. The area around the Ballydorn–Castlehalbert Road is cow and sheep country, little farms laid like a bumpy

26

stone quilt on the slopes of the Silver Ridge. I could have been at any one of the thirty or forty small farms within a nine or ten-mile radius – but who is to say we were that close? The small farms are fewer and farther between as you go up into the Silver Ridge, where they are isolated whitewashed stone buildings nestled at the end of long winding lanes – and I can't remember anything that would help to pick out one place in particular.

"You must be able to estimate how long it took to get there," the police kept saying to me, which is a bit of extraordinary double-thinking on their part, considering that their van disposal theory has me unconscious during the journey! I have no idea how long that first journey took. It could have been twenty minutes, or an hour, or two hours. I was so scared and confused that I just haven't a clue. It is even possible that we weren't up on the slopes of the Silver Ridge at all.

The next thing I remember is Dodie loosening the blanket around my head. It was held by a hangman's noose around my throat, the rest of the blanket covering me like a shroud. There was a rope outside the blanket, around my middle, pinning my arms to my sides. My hands were tied together, and my feet were roped as well at my ankles. I don't remember being tied up, so maybe there is something in the police theory that I was unconscious during part of the first journey.

Anyway, Dodie loosened the ropes, but she didn't remove the blanket from my head.

"There," a woman's voice said. "There now, you're all right, dear. Lie still."

The Woman's voice is a problem to me. Later, when the police were trying to find out where she lived and who she was, they took me to three or four remote farms and kept me in the back of their car so I could hear as they interviewed people. But none of the voices were anything like the Woman's. I must be the most useless witness to anything they ever had. They told me they had a good idea who it was, but when I couldn't help on time or physical detail or the sound of the Woman's voice, there wasn't much they could do.

At the time, I wasn't worried about being a witness. All I registered was that the voice was one I hadn't heard before, much less squeaky than the voice of the girl who'd been trying to calm me down in the van. It was a female voice, but there was nothing particular about it that I can remember, except that it had a real edge of anger to it. She was being nice to me but, by the tone of her voice, she was frightened and anxious as well. I had the impression that the voice didn't belong to a young woman, but I have nothing at all to back that up with.

"If you thrash about like that, you'll hurt yourself," she said reprovingly.

"Bloody bitch!" said Leo, and he prodded my side with the toe of his boot. I know it was him. After listening to him cursing away in the van, there was no way I could forget his voice.

"You're lucky she isn't badly hurt," the Woman said. "Be careful, or you'll do her damage."

"She's asking for it, isn't she?" from Leo.

"You've got to get rid of her," the Woman said. "She can't stay here. None of you are staying here, for that matter."

"What are we supposed to do?"

"You can make tracks," the Woman said. "One thing I do know: you are not keeping her here; you've got to dump her somewhere."

"We can't."

"You're going to have to. I'm not letting her be found up here."

"She knows me!" came from Leo, with a touch of whine in his voice.

"Don't do that!" said the Woman's voice urgently. I don't know what she saved me from.

"Another squeak out of her and I will!"

"Not here you won't," said the Woman. "You, her, your two friends, the lot of you. I want you out of here, now, Leo."

I registered the *Leo*. They'd given me two names, Dodie and Leo, to work on – though neither name meant anything to me. Giving away the names like that just shows how bad they were at handling things.

Then there was a string of what Mrs Flynn down the road from us at home would call badmouthing from Leo. The Woman, whoever she was, wasn't having any of that.

"Get outa here!" she yelled. "Do you hear me now? Get outa here and on your way. And don't be laying your troubles at my door!"

"Jesus, woman— "

"You've really done it, this time!" the Woman said. "And if you hurt that wee girl, you'll only make it worse."

Then I heard a door. I think it was a sliding door, because of the creaks and squeaks it made, but I have no way of knowing where it led to.

That was the end of that conversation, and of the Woman as far as I am concerned. She could have set me free, or at the very least she could have phoned the police after they'd cleared off if she was too scared to intervene. I don't think she was all that scared. She sounded as if she was just worried for herself, not me, or them for that matter. She didn't want to be found with a victim lying around the place, that's all.

Mum says if she ever lays hands on that woman, she'll kill her, which is pure Mum-talk really. Mum has always had energy to burn, and some of it she has passed on to her offspring. I suppose it was in part being like

Mum that pulled me through.

Just then I didn't feel like Mum. I felt like a rag doll.

They left me alone and I thrashed about, which got me nowhere. That was followed by a good cry and, after that, I just lay for I don't know how long, intensely cramped and uncomfortable, and conscious of the dried blood caked around my nose.

Then the sliding door again and steps.

"I think she can maybe see us through that thing," came nervously from Dodie, and I felt her hands working at the blanket around my head.

"I'll fix that!" said Leo.

"She might get that stuff off," Dodie said.

"There's no way she'll get it off!"

"Mmmmmm!" I mumbled apprehensively. It was bad enough being tied up as I was.

"We've decided to take this blanket off you," Dodie said close to my ear. "You're to keep your eyes shut when we do. Understood? We're going to tape your eyes up so you can't see us, but you'll have the blanket off your head and you'll be more comfortable."

"Mmmmmm!" from me.

"No peeking!" from the girl.

Then the blanket came off and I did as I was told because I was afraid of what they might do to me if I didn't. That is it. In that kind of situation you don't waste time, and I didn't.

It was old sticky tape, the brown tacky sort that people use for heavy parcels. Leo wrapped it around and around and around my eyes umpteen times.

"She's all messed with blood," Dodie said. "Maybe I should— "

"Never bother," Leo said. "Time enough for that later on."

"Mmmmmmm! Mmmmmmmmmmmmm!"

"Shut up you, or he might hurt you!" Dodie whispered close in my ear.

So I shut up.

Then Leo tightened the bonds the girl had loosened, and they carted me between them like a sack of potatoes. I was dumped into the back seat of a car, which I now know was an old Toyota.

Leo got in the back with me. The other one, Gerard, didn't seem to be there. The girl was doing the driving again.

"Do we go left at the end of the lane?" I heard Dodie ask.

"No talk about where we're headed!" Leo said. "We don't want Suzie Q hearing stuff she might repeat later."

Bound, blindfolded, gagged, and en route to I had no idea what awful fate, I still managed to pick up the really life-threatening bit.

Suzie Q.

My own personal private family name: *Suzie Q.*

If he knew enough about our family affairs to know that, he had to be local. If he was local enough to know me, it was probable that I did know him, at least by sight. He thought I'd seen him and that I could trot around and identify him to the police the moment they let me go.

Which is why they weren't going to.

CHAPTER FIVE

There never was anything funny-ha-ha about my being kidnapped or held hostage or whatever you want to call it. The whole experience was mind-shattering and horrendous for me and my family and our neighbours, the Flynns. Nevertheless, black comedy kept intervening all the way through.

The first ludicrous bit was Ruth's rescue from the Manure Man.

Ruth, you will remember, was to be picked up from the bus at Kilturn crossroads, but when the bus dropped her off there with her overnight bag, there was no sign of Mum or me or the car.

Ruth was duly annoyed.

There she was after a bus and train journey all the way from Belfast, dumped by the side of a ditch in the middle of nowhere, and apparently facing a long *plod, plod, plod* on the eight-mile road to Cloughanny, which is a long way from the civilized world.

Her first thought, not unnaturally, was to settle down by the ditch and wait. She thought we must have been held up and we'd be along in a minute.

The minutes went by, and no sign of our car.

Ruth knew we couldn't have got the days mixed up, because she was due home for Davie's birthday. That was the whole purpose of her coming, and Davie's birthday was the next day, and there are only two Long Route buses that drop off near Cloughanny. Even if we'd thought she was due on the early one, which goes by about eleven-fifteen in the morning, she obviously hadn't been on it, so she had to be on the five-to-five, and we should have been there to meet her.

Ten-past five, and a police car went by, going full speed. Ruth didn't know why it was in such a hurry, or where it was going.

Twenty-past, and she was fed up, so she got up and put her long legs to work. Ruth gets her long legs from our dad. I'm stunted like Mum. When Mum and Dad got married, somebody made some crack about the Big Man getting his wife out of a cornflake box. The way it worked out with them, though, was Mum had the strength and Dad had the look of it. She really proved that strength when he died, just before Davie was born.

Anyway, Ruth got her reluctant legs to go, on the theory that Mum must have been way-laid by her electorate, or caught behind a herd of cows, and Ruth should better start walking. She fully expected to meet our car coming up the road.

She'd gone about a mile and a quarter, lugging her big floppy bag, when a car came up behind her.

We're not supposed to hitch, but Ruth was tired out after the bus ride and she didn't fancy miles and miles of winding road, so she gave the car the thumb.

It wasn't much of a car. She says it looked as if it was held together with string and a prayer, and there was a man in it, but he looked a harmless wee man and she wasn't worried.

So she got her lift, and they started talking.

She told him she was in her second year at Queen's, which is the university in Belfast, studying English. She's still thrilled at having made it and she tells everybody that. She was always university material, but she had a rocky year or two when Dad died and Mum was pre-occupied with sorting things out, and her bad bit coincided with her GCSEs, which she blew. The school was in two minds when she turned up for her A level year saying she wanted to go to university, but Mum had been dinning it into her that she had to sort her life out, and

Ruth really buttoned down. She got good grades and made it, so she has a right to be proud.

Then it was the man's turn.

"I'm in manure," he told her, just like that.

She says he didn't mean it to be funny. He was a no-sense-of-humour kind of wee man.

He started giving her a manure lecture.

They were discussing the biological activity of microbes in cow dung, as modified by the latest EC regulations, or something like that, when they came around one of the bends in the road and found themselves confronted by the British Army.

That puzzles me too. How did the army get there so quickly? There were no vehicles, so they hadn't come by road. Mum thinks they may just have been patrolling in the area and received a call from the police. This must sound weird to people who don't live in Northern Ireland, but it is a fact of life here that we have small units of soldiers, armed to the teeth, out creeping around the fields and dodging behind hedges trying to catch the IRA. They are heli-coptered in and helicoptered out. They are sup-posed to be there for Anti-Terrorist Operations, but when something happens like Suzie Q – kidnapped-by-robbers, they tend to be pulled in.

So ... a soldier in the road with a rifle, full combat gear, his face smeared with camouflage blackout, hand raised to stop the car. Beyond him there was one in the ditch with their radio. There were three or four more in the hedge and some close to the road, in the fields on either side.

At least three of them had their guns trained on the car.

The Manure Man pulled out his driver's licence and rolled the window down.

The soldier gave him the usual "where are you going, sir" line of chat, and took the licence from him.

Meanwhile, the one kneeling down by the hedge with the radio had noted the car number and was busy radioing it in, to check that the vehicle wasn't on the risk register.

All of that was normal enough in our war zone.

Then another soldier – Ruth thinks this one was an officer – came out of the hedge from behind the car, on the passenger side. He said something to the first one over the roof of the car.

"Would you mind stepping out of the car, sir?" the first soldier said to the Manure Man.

As the Manure Man climbed out, the officer came up on Ruth's side of the car and tapped the window.

Ruth rolled the window down.

The officer stood looking at her, but he didn't say anything until the soldier got his body between the Manure Man and the car. The soldier was making a great fuss about opening the boot – more of a fuss than usual, Ruth thought.

The officer bent down and put his head through the open window. "Are you all right, Miss?" he said to Ruth softly.

By this time Ruth knew something was up.

It is a funny thing about the British soldiers over here. They are nice enough most of the time to most people, but they have a way of making you *feel* guilty, as though you've done something even when you haven't. That is particularly true when they stop you on the road. They have every right to be scared and apprehensive, because so many of them have been murdered, but they try to act superconfident and in control, even though they must be shivering inside. Every car they stop *might* contain a terrorist who *might* be about to pull a gun on them, and so they are keyed up inside. When they start asking you questions, their feelings somehow transmit to you … they are *expecting* you to pull something, because they have to think that way, from a sense of self-preservation.

The odd way this officer came at Ruth, whispering through the window, made her think she was in trouble. She says she was convinced the Manure Man had a stack of guns in the boot, or he was on the run, and now she was going to be arrested as an accessory after

39

the fact or something.

The upshot was that instead of saying something cheery like "I'm right as rain" to the officer, Ruth said, "I'll be all right when I'm out of here," meaning that she didn't like the situation. But she thinks she sounded a bit nervous, which of course she was.

She says his eyes changed suddenly.

"Miss Quinn?" he said.

"Yes," she said, wondering how on earth he knew her name.

The next thing she knew, three soldiers had the Manure Man spread-eagled on the road with a gun to his head!

He was yelling blue murder and the soldiers were carrying on as if they had won the Alamo and the officer was telling her she was safe now, Miss, and they wouldn't let the bastard near her.

Ruth couldn't make it out, but she is great on Human Rights. She has an Amnesty badge and all that stuff, and the way they were going on at the Manure Man made her forget about the possibility of his being a terrorist. She says she was sure he wasn't anyway, and she felt she couldn't stand by and see an innocent man abused like that.

"What are you doing to that wee man?" Ruth demanded. "Why are they treating him like that?"

"You're all right now, dear," said the officer.

By the time she was out of the car and on the

side of the road, the soldiers had the Manure Man lying with his arms spread out and his nose tight to the tar, prodding him with their rifles.

"Well, you can't do that to anybody, you know!" Ruth said, coming on fiercely. "There's still a law in this land, whatever you may think!"

The officer must have thought she'd gone around the bend.

We think he'd only heard part of the story over his radio, and that part was to concentrate on rescuing a Miss Quinn who'd been involved as a hostage in a hold-up.

Now, with Ruth backing up the Manure Man, he got the notion in his head that the story was wrong and this Miss Quinn who was mouthing at him hadn't been kidnapped at all – Miss Quinn was part of the gang. He started yelling questions at her and she was yelling Civil Liberty stuff back at him while the poor Manure Man was sweating it out, face down in the road.

In the course of a heated conversation Ruth admits that she called the officer some terrible names, and then she began to catch herself because you don't mess with the army and she took another tack, threatening to tell her mother, the local Councillor.

That's the moment when her mother, the local Councillor, came roaring up the road in a police car, thinking she was about to get Quinn daughter number two back, only to find Quinn daughter number one threatening the soldiers with all sorts of legal action on behalf of the Manure Man.

"Where is she? Where is she?" cried Mum, meaning me.

"Mum, this animal's a rude pig!" cried Ruth, meaning the officer. "His backside needs kicking."

"That's it," said the officer to Ruth. "You're under arrest."

"You take your hands off my daughter!" screamed Mum, who was in a bad enough way about losing one daughter, without having the other one arrested by the army.

Drama and histrionics! Mum going off like a firecracker, Ruth trying to comfort her and take in what had happened at the same time, the officer trying to arrest Ruth as an accomplice kidnapper and the police trying to explain that she wasn't, and the poor Manure Man muttering "Can I get off this road?" at intervals, and nobody paying him attention except the soldier who was holding the gun to his neck.

Ruth says that is the last time she will hitch a lift, and it is certainly the last time the Manure Man will give anybody one. It's also the last time any British Army Officer will risk his neck exchanging words with my mum. It wasn't his fault at all, he'd been doing the right thing, but apparently he caught the end of Mum's tongue in no uncertain fashion.

CHAPTER SIX

I was at the quarry on Stonecutters Mountain.

As the police pointed out to me later, it is no place for a family picnic. There are no fences around the old quarry, because there are no people to guard against. The only way to get there is along a rough track that goes through miles of heather, rocks, and nothingness. The quarry lies abandoned on one side of a steeply sloping valley between two small mountains, Black Cap and Stonecutters, and the initial slopes of the Silver Ridge range rise up in front of it, making it into an enclosed low-lying pocket in very high ground, the kind of place that is lost in mist most of the winter. When I came later with the police, we jolted for miles and miles on what was left of the rough track, without seeing even one tumbledown cottage, which is most unusual for Ireland, but probably accounted for by the extremes of the weather up there and the very inhospitable nature of the rock and sparse heather surroundings. The quarry was used during the construction of the Seeley Dam in the Silver Ridge when they were making the Seeley Reservoir as a feeder for the big reservoir at Passenger's Lake. When the work was completed, there was no further use for the quarry, because it was too far out of the way of civilization to serve any practical purpose, so it was abandoned.

In other words it was an almost impossible place to get to, and, by the same token, almost impossible to get away from, unless you happened to be a mountain goat.

I didn't know then where I was, only that I'd come a long way, and the last part had been bone-rattlingly bad, so that it was a big relief when we came to the end of the second journey of my captivity. I was left alone for a while, presumably while they made their initial arrangements, and then they lifted me out of the car.

They dumped me on rocky ground and untied my ankles and legs. Then they unwound the sticky tape from around my head. There were three figures standing over me, silhouetted against the night sky.

There was something odd about them that took me a moment or two to take in.

Two of them had no heads!

44

That was what it looked like, and then I realized they *had* heads, but their heads were covered in plastic shopping bags with slits for their eyes and mouths. The third one had his head encased in a motorcycle helmet, painted bright red with BIG G on it in yellow-glow lettering. He had a scarf pulled up to cover his mouth and nose.

Thinking about it now, the BIG G was a typical Gerard mistake, considering that he was hoping to keep his identity secret by wearing it. At the time, I didn't know his name, so it didn't register.

I think they removed the sticky tape because I wouldn't be able to walk over the rough ground properly if I couldn't see, and they didn't fancy carrying me. The shopping bags and the BIG G helmet were the best identity-preservers they could come up with at short notice.

"Get her up!" Leo said. There was no mistaking that voice. It gave me the shivers.

The two boys pulled me up on to my feet.

"Walk!" Leo shouted at me.

"Don't shout at her. That isn't going to do any good!" I heard from Dodie.

Of course I couldn't walk. When they let go of me, I just keeled over and sat down. My legs were very painful and totally useless as things for moving about on, which isn't surprising considering how securely they'd been bound up.

"We'll have to lug her after all!" Leo said, sounding disgusted. I don't know what he'd been expecting.

"Give him a hand, Gerard," Dodie said.

Gerard. Gerard and Leo and Dodie. They'd given me all three names in conversation, despite all the stuff about concealing their identities. I remember registering how stupid they must be.

They heaved me up between them and dragged me along. It turned into more of a stagger than a walk, with one of the boys on either side supporting me, their arms crooked under my armpits, and Dodie steering me from the back.

I had time to take in that we were high up. I could hardly miss that because of the bleak outline of the mountains against the night sky, and the extreme cold, but I had no idea where I was apart from that, just up a mountain and heading for a squat two-storey stone house, picked out by the dull light of a storm lamp shining in one of the bottom windows.

They didn't take me into the lighted room.

There was a rough stone hut built on to one end of the house, about six feet high, with a rusty tin roof and a heavy timber door. It looked like the kind of half-tumbled hovel people keep goats tethered in.

They pushed me in through the door and then slammed and bolted it.

"I'll bring you a blanket!" Dodie shouted through the closed door. And then I heard their footsteps departing around the end of the hut.

So there I was, totally terrified and confused, lying on the cobbled floor of a freezing cold goat hut, with my legs and ankles free but my arms still tightly tied.

I wound myself into the foetal position on the floor and lay there. My clothes were stinking because I'd messed myself somewhere along the way, which is not surprising considering the state of fear they'd put me in – people do lose control and there was nothing I could do to prevent it. I don't even know exactly when it happened, but it had, and I hated the idea of it.

I thought that Dodie would come with the promised blanket and some food and water for me, maybe even clean me up a bit, but she didn't. No one came near me at all.

She never did explain that to me properly. I believed her when she said she *meant* to do it, but she said that they had a few beer cans with them and they made a small fire and then they had a can or two and Leo and Gerard started arguing. She was caught up in it, taking Gerard's side because she always had to – Gerard not being hot stuff at standing up for his own opinions. Apparently, things got pretty unpleasant. Leo was shouting and bawling at them, telling them they were spineless, and going on about having to do all their thinking for them.

"I suppose I just forgot you," she said. "I was upset for Gerard. Leo kept calling him names."

As a result, I spent my first night in the goat hut on Stonecutters Mountain completely alone and in total darkness, with my clothes dirty and blood-soaked all the way down the front, and my poor body frozen to the bone. It was a long, long night, but lying there in the darkness gave me a lot of time and, despite everything, I made myself think, and plan.

That's like Mum again.

Mum says that in my position she would have curled up and died and not done anything, but I don't think so. Mum isn't like that. She never lets things overwhelm her. She has a thing about getting up and fighting when she finds herself in real trouble, and she must have passed it on to me.

I knew I had to plan, and fight, if necessary, but I couldn't imagine how I was going to do it.

Ruth says Mum was doing the same at home.

Mum wanted to fight, but there wasn't anything she could think of to do.

By that stage, the story was out on the radio and TV and I was on my way to being KIDNAP GIRL SUZIE Q, 15 and all that stuff, plastered over the tabloids next morning, while my nearest and dearest were condemned to sitting

48

in the house and waiting.

They had their own personally assigned policewoman standing by on the premises. She was called Margaret Campbell. Margaret was red-haired and in her thirties, and turned out to be a good person, but she got off on the wrong foot with Mum and Ruth, telling them to "call me Margaret" and acting generally as if they were helpless. Mum and Ruth are both fierce people, with heads on their shoulders, and they felt they were being patronized.

Margaret had been trained to deal with families in distress. Ruth says that means she'd passed all the exams and read all the books. She was sweet and firm and understanding, and she nearly drove them mad because they didn't want her there. Margaret had the intelligence to see that her approach wasn't working, so she concentrated on doing what she could about Davie. Mum and Ruth were trying to keep the upset from him, but of course he was wise to the fact that something was wrong, even if he didn't know what it was. The policewoman sat for ages in his room, reading to him, although all the time she had the door open, ready to pounce on the telephone if it rang.

Of course, Davie wouldn't go to sleep without Mum.

Mum went in and took over from Margaret, and that put the policewoman in our living room with Ruth.

They talked about this and that for a while, though Ruth says she was very conscious of the other woman being professional all the time, gleaning little bits of information with casual questions.

Ruth got sick of it.

"Look, if you don't mind, Margaret, we'd feel better on our own," Ruth said to her in the end. "My sister is the one who is in danger. Mum and I aren't. Really we need to be on our own in our own house."

"I'm afraid I have to stay here in the house," Margaret told her firmly.

"Why?" Ruth wanted to know.

"Somebody might try to contact you or Suzie might turn up," Margaret said, putting a good face on it. "I'm here to help you look after your mother, and the little boy."

Positive again, you see. Forming a bond with the people in trouble, putting herself in Ruth's shoes, but preparing her for the worst just in case. It was totally absurd, of course, because Mum isn't the kind of person people look after. Mum would have had policewoman Margaret fried on toast for supper if she'd heard her. Mum was all grim-lipped and tense, ready for the fight. I'd back her against any policewoman in coping with an emergency. If anyone was in danger of going weepy, it was Ruth herself.

Ruth made up her mind that Margaret was trying to talk to her in code words, so she gave it to her straight on, just to show that she wasn't stupid.

"In case our Suzie Q turns up dead, you mean?" Ruth said brutally.

"Well, not exactly," Margaret said.

"If Suzie turns up alive, there won't be any coping to do," Ruth said. "Unless they hurt her someway." She says she had all sorts of horrors in her mind about what my kidnappers might have done to me. Mum felt the same, and they wanted to talk to each other about it, but they couldn't bring themselves to do it in front of Margaret. They felt they were performing for her benefit, and they didn't want to end up as psychological footnotes in her exam for Sergeant.

"I'm very sorry, Margaret," Ruth said eventually. "I understand you are only doing your duty, but my mother and I need to be alone for a while, like *now*. Just with each other. So maybe you wouldn't mind if we asked you to go into the kitchen, while we have a talk in here."

Margaret said "Yes, of course" in her best trained professional voice, if that was what Ruth wanted.

Then she went and sat in the kitchen, looking at the fridge for entertainment.

Ruth brought the little portable TV in for

her and made her some instant coffee and biscuits, by which time Mum had appeared from the bedroom, having finally got Davie to sleep.

"If the phone goes, you'll hear it first in here," Ruth told Margaret, and she went back to the living room, where Mum was sitting fretting.

So they ended up with this trained Social Worker Type Policewoman watching *Newsnight* in our kitchen, ready to spring at the telephone if it rung, while they sat and gritted their combined teeth in the living room.

"What will we do if they come demanding ransom money?" Ruth asked Mum.

"It was only young children that took her," Mum said. "Two young boys about your age."

"Just the same… " Ruth said.

"If I thought it would save our Suzie Q, they'd get their money," Mum said.

"We have no money," Ruth pointed out.

"We'd get it some way," Mum said, very determined. "We could raise some money on the house, maybe."

"The police wouldn't let us pay up. They'd want to play some fancy trick so the kidnappers would get caught collecting it. They wouldn't let us just pay it over in the hope that we'd get her back safe, no questions asked," Ruth said.

They sat there for a long time discussing

how they might get money, but they didn't really come up with anything. Mum teaches in the five-teacher primary school in Cloughanny, which doesn't pay much, and the only thing we have is the house. Dad had an endowment policy on the mortgage that paid out when he died, so Mum owns it. But owning it and raising money against it quickly would be two different things.

"It wouldn't be millions of pounds they'd be after, if they are only young ones," Ruth said. "They'd know we haven't millions, if they had any sense."

"I'd give them anything they wanted, if it would get her back," Mum said. "And if that means deceiving the police, then I'd do that too." There was desperation in her voice. Ruth says she's never seen Mum like that before.

"Maybe they'll just turn Suzie loose from wherever they've got her," Ruth said, trying to turn down the heat.

"That's what I'm hoping," Mum said, and then she started crying.

It was the only time she did break down completely. It scared the wits out of Ruth.

I'd be interested to know if anyone contacted policewoman Margaret on her little radio to tell her about the van being found. If they did, she must have decided on her own initiative not to tell Mum and Ruth.

Possibly it was because of the blood in the

back of the van and the feeling that any minute they might come up with a body.

The fact that their investigations had led them to the wrong conclusion – that I was dead, and in the lake, and that my abductors were miles away – is neither here nor there.

I think Mum should have been told that night, however late it was when they got the information. So does Mum, as she informed them in no uncertain terms when policewoman Margaret finally got around to breaking the news to her.

I gather there were little bits of policewoman Margaret all over the floor by the time Mum had finished with her.

CHAPTER SEVEN

At least Mum and Ruth had each other to talk to. I had a long night all by myself.

It was morning when Dodie finally turned up and unlocked the padlock on my hutch. She had abandoned the plastic shopping bag and was wearing a pillowcase over her head and shoulders, with eye slits cut in it.

"You all right, Suzie Q?" she asked, coming through the door. "I've come to clean you up."

My pet name again, *Suzie Q*.

"Mmmmmmm," from me through the gag.

She had a bucket with her, and a sponge and a towel.

"Cheer up, Suzie," she said. "I'll clean you up, won't I?"

She was speaking down to me as if I was a child, and I *was* child-helpless, with my arms bound by my sides.

"You are a mess!" she told me. "Never

mind! Soon have you all lovely again!"

I let her do it, although it was humiliating and upsetting and degrading, all those things. I had no choice. She got my jeans and under-things off and washed me, and then she went off and came back with some clean stuff. She put fresh jeans on me. They were about two sizes too big.

"Now then!" she said, sitting back on her haunches, head bent so that she wouldn't bang it on the roof. "Feel any better now, Suzie Q?"

"Mmmmmmmm," I nodded.

"I'm going to get you some hot food," she said. Then she added, almost coyly, "Don't run away on me now!"

Ha-bloody-ha! was my internal reaction, but I let her have a nod of assent, just to keep her happy, though it went against the grain. Given an even chance, I'd have cheerfully throttled her – but there was no even chance. If my immediate survival depended on devel-oping a relationship of some bizarre kind with a robber's moll who wandered around the place dressed up like a Munchkin, then that was what I was going to do. It is what Mum calls making the most of limited resources.

I got the video of *The Wizard of Oz* out for Davie one time, and there were lots of little Munchkins in it. They used midgets, and Ruth was furious. She said that she thought using them in the film was exploitation, which is what she would say. Our Ruth is always politically correct. Anyway, that's what the girl looked like with the pillowcase over her head and shoulders. A small fat Munchkin in *The Wizard of Oz.*

She came back with some soup in a can for me. The can was rough-edged around the top, and hot, so that she had to hold it with a towel wrapped around her hand.

"Soup, Suzie? Nice soup?"

The gag had to come off so that I could take the soup. It was an immense relief to me.

"No shouting, Suzie," she warned, before she unwound the gag. "It wouldn't do you any good. There is no one to hear you."

I nodded. I'd had the night to think about it, and I'd already arrived at the conclusion that I had to play everything low-key because I was completely at their mercy.

"There you are," she said, removing the gag. "Not so bad, is it? Now you have that old thing off you."

There was blood on the side of the gag, and my mouth hurt terribly. The skin was raw at the corners where the gag had been pulled tight.

"My mouth hurts," I told her. My voice came out all croaky. "I am freezing cold, numb with it. You've got to warm me up."

"You'll feel better when you've eaten something hot," she said.

She started to feed me as best she could in the absence of a spoon, which meant holding the soup can up to my lips.

"My arms hurt even more," I told her. "I think you've done something to my circulation."

"I know," she said. "But Leo won't let us untie you. Gerard asked, but he said no."

"Do you two always do what Leo says?"

Long pause.

"Look. I can't *do* anything if you untie me," I said. "You've got me, haven't you?"

"Yeh," she said.

"I promise I won't try anything," I said. It was no big deal, really, giving my word. I knew I couldn't have managed to get twenty yards if she'd untied me and told me to run for it, not that she was likely to do that.

"Well... " she said doubtfully.

"*Please,*" I said, "Look ... it really *hurts*. My arms are all cramped, tied up this way. And there's something wrong with my shoulder. And I'm so cold that I can hardly feel most of the bits of me."

I wasn't trying to kid her. I felt cold and sick and weak and my shoulder was very *very* painful. It must have happened one of the times when they dumped me down. "Heavy bruising" was how the doctors described it later, but at the time, I thought I must have chipped a bone.

58

"It's all swollen up," she said, reaching her hand out towards me as she said it.

"Don't touch it!" I said quickly.

"All right," she said doubtfully. "I'll untie you, for a bit. But I'll have to tie you up again later, Suzie, mind you."

And she untied me.

You've no idea of the relief … though it was painful when I tried to move. I managed to sit up, and, after a bit of massaging, I took the can from her and started on the soup. It was very watery and tasteless, but piping hot. I imagine their cooking resources were limited to a camping stove, or something like that.

She backed away from me and waited by the door, fretting, which was plain silly of her, because she must have known that I wasn't strong enough to tackle her. I had no illusions about that. My mind was working, but my body was in a bad way – being trussed up like a Christmas turkey tends to leave you debilitated.

I made short work of the soup, but I didn't want to be tied up again, so I decided to have a go at conversation, on the theory that she might be the weak link I could win over to my side.

"I don't understand why you are keeping me."

No reply.

"There'll be police and army searches going

59

on," I said. "They're bound to find me sooner or later. Why don't you let me go?"

"You saw Leo," she said. "You saw his face in the van when you pulled his scarf down. When you were fighting. Before he hit you." Then she added, "I'm sorry he hit you."

"I didn't see his face – not really," I said. "It was all too quick."

"You would say that," she said. "But you saw him just the same. He says you know him, and you saw his face, Suzie Q."

Pause, while I thought about that.

"I didn't see him," I said. "I *really* didn't. Even if I had, I wouldn't be able to recognize him again, honestly. I don't think I've ever seen him before anyway."

"You know fine well who Leo is," she said, confirming what I'd already worked out. I didn't know who he was, but he *thought* I did, which meant that he knew me, or the crowd I moved in, or Mum, sufficiently well to believe that I would be able to pin an identity on him.

"He won't do anything bad to you," she added, probably reading my feelings from my expression. "We wouldn't let him. You weren't supposed to be in it. It wasn't supposed to be like this at all. It's all gone wrong. It's just another old mess, as if I wasn't messed up enough already."

I didn't pick up on that remark at the time; it seemed to be only a throwaway moan, but it was significant.

"You won't get hurt, Suzie, believe me," she repeated, sounding a bit desperate. "You've nothing to worry about."

In the circumstances it wasn't very convincing, and the look I gave her must have told her so.

"I've told Leo not to hurt you," she went on, sounding really doleful and a bit panic-stricken. "I'm out if he hurts you, right?"

Again silence from me. Letting her talk seemed the best policy. It might even get her thinking about letting me go.

"This is all just a terrible silly mistake!" she burst out. "I absolutely don't want you to suffer for it, because you haven't done anything and you're not even meant to be here. I'm really very sorry it has all worked out like this. Only now you are here and we've got you, and we are in big trouble and we just don't know what to do with you."

I could have shaken her. They'd got me. They didn't want me. There was no point in holding on to me. They didn't know what to do with me, and so they were just going to sit there until the police showed up, as they surely would. Then it would be panic stations.

"It won't be like it is on TV," I said slowly. "If you try holding me hostage to do a deal with the police, it will all end in a mess, and somebody will be killed." *Probably me* was the thought in my mind, but I didn't say it.

Long pause.

"They have to find us first," she said. "Nobody comes up here."

"Where is here?" I asked.

No reply.

"We can't stay where we are forever, however well hidden and out of the way it is," I said.

"I know that," she said.

"You know what I think?" I went on. "You'll have to drop me off in some remote spot and drive on your way. By the time I've managed to raise the alarm, you could be through the roadblocks and over the border into the Republic, where the police won't be looking for you."

Another long pause.

"You really will have to let me go, sooner or later," I said. "Can't you see that?"

"You saw Leo. You know who he is," she said despairingly. "He won't let you go."

"I don't know him. But if I did, it wouldn't make much difference, would it? Once you are over the border, you would be OK."

It wasn't true, of course, but it fitted the ideas she was used to. The police on the Republic of Ireland side would be just as anxious to prove how great they were as the Northern Ireland Security Forces would be. There's a big myth about lack of co-operation between the authorities in Northern Ireland, which is the British side, and the Republic, which is the officially Irish bit, but even the myth doesn't extend to the kind of kidnapping mess those three had got themselves into.

"So long as you keep hold of me, the police will be excited about it," I said. "If you let me go, who cares? Who is going to be *really* bothered if you get away after robbing Danny Semple of a few quid from his till? Nobody!"

Long silence, while I let her take that on board.

"Leo says they're all searching for us," she said. Obviously I got under her skin. She started repeating a "Leo-says" mantra, as if repeating it would make it come true. "Police and Army and TV and everybody. But Leo says we're safe as long as we're hidden here, because nobody ever comes up this high."

"That's nonsense!" I said tartly, realizing as I did it that I was making a mistake. I was supposed to be sympathetic, not critical.

She picked up on it immediately.

"Listen," she said. "You think you are in a mess over this business, don't you?"

"I am," I said. "Look at me!"

"Well, you're not the only one," she said. "I'd just like you to know that I'm left with my little life totally jiggered by all this, and none of it is my fault!"

Impasse.

I didn't know what to say. How could it not be her fault, any of it, when she had set off to rob a store and ended up as an assistant kidnapper?

"I've got to tie you up again," she said, rallying.

"*Got* to?"

"Going to," she amended. "Only I won't tie you as tight as before, so it won't hurt much."

"Thanks a bundle," I said.

She was as good as her word. She tied me up so that I counted as tied up, but the ropes didn't hurt, and she never bothered with the gag. I believe Dodie when she says she wanted to make things as easy as she could for me. She had to balance that against her fear of Leo and she found it difficult, not being a natural prison warden.

"There," she said. "I'll bring something warm to wrap you up in, to keep out the cold. A few old coats or a duvet or something."

She was as good as her word, but she didn't stay with me or talk to me again for hours. She says it was big conference time for them, and she was afraid to talk to me too much in case she gave things away.

I was left for hours and hours lying on the floor, tied up and wrapped in an old duvet. I can still feel the cobbles as they pressed into my side, and see the chinks of light coming through the rotten old tin roof. The whole place was dank and musty and stinking, as well as being freezing cold.

Back at home, reluctant Margaret had broken the news about the discovery of the half-burnt-out van up at Plumber's Point. I suppose she had to tell them before word leaked out to the radio and press people.

By then, the police had carried out forensic tests, and the tests confirmed that the stains in the back of the van were blood, which made them think murder.

To establish that it was a murder case, they needed to be sure it was my blood.

It seems to me that any policeman worth his salt would have darted around to the local GP and discreetly got hold of my medical records, but, incredible as it seems, that isn't what they did.

The phone rang at our house.

Ruth was on her own at home and she answered it.

Did she know her sister Suzie's blood type, because they'd got hold of the van and there was blood in the back.

Not unnaturally, Ruth's mind reeled at that, because the implications were obvious.

"No, I don't know," she said.

"Would your mother know, perhaps?" came the police voice at the end of the line.

Quick thinking by Ruth, who could imagine

the reaction if she told Mum they were checking out bloodstains in the van.

"There's no way I'm asking her that! Anyway, she's not here. She's gone down to the school with your police lady in tow."

"Well, we need to know."

Ruth said they'd have the record at Thomas Bragen Hospital, where I'd had my tonsils out.

"Oh," from the voice, sounding disconcerted. The voice seemed to think for a bit, then it rallied. "The medical people are very fussy with their red tape on these matters. Are you sure Mrs Quinn wouldn't know? Maybe you could ask your mother to contact us when she gets back?"

Ruth says she only just held her temper.

"I'm not asking my mother a question like that at a time like this!"

End of telephone call.

Once Ruth had dried her tears and straightened her face out, she was left thinking: *How am I going to tell Mum that the police believe Suzie is dead?*

Then mum arrived back, with our personal policewoman in the passenger seat.

Mum marched into the house with a face like death on her.

"They found the van, Ruth," Mum said, straight out. "There was blood all over the back."

I can't forgive the police for that. There

wasn't blood all over the back of the van, just some from my cut leg and my bloody nose. They let Mum and Ruth live with the impression that there were buckets of the stuff. I suppose the police have a lot to do. Maybe neither the voice on the telephone that spoke to Ruth nor whichever one contacted Mum down at the school thought through what effect their words would have, but they should have.

My mum and my sister were put through the mill, and all for nothing – as if things weren't grim enough for them already.

I suppose the police were doing their best and I'm sure they believed they were going about it in the right way, but it really annoys me that Mum was never consulted or involved in their decisions, or kept properly informed about what was happening.

Mum is clever and intelligent and resourceful. She could have helped them, and instead she was treated as an hysterical half-wit most of the time, and kept well away from the people who were making all the decisions.

My kidnappers took a different line. They were determined to involve me.

CHAPTER EIGHT

It was Gerard who brought me out of the hut and around the front of the house.

He didn't say much, just that they wanted to have a talk with me, to try and sort some things out. He had taken the ropes off my arms, but my wrists were still tied, and he had fixed a kind of hobble rope leading from one ankle to the other to stop me from having a rush of blood to the head and suddenly running off. Thankfully there was no return to the gag or the blanket-over-the-head business.

I think Leo wanted me to see where I was, so that I would grasp the impossibility of escaping from it.

The house was derelict. I could see that it was part of a quarry, but obviously one that wasn't in use anymore. There are quite a few of those around Silver Ridge, so that didn't help me sort out where I was, except that I wasn't anywhere I'd been before. Grey stone was in piles all over the place, and tons and tons of shale, the whole thing sticking out on the side of the mountain like a sore thumb.

My instant impression was that there was an awful lot of mountain around me and very little else – no sign of any other human habitation, just the abandoned workings.

I got my first sight of the car and, more interestingly, of an old motorcycle, heavily painted in red, with lightning down the side. It clicked in my head that the lovingly painted motorcycle matched the red racing helmet with BIG G on it that my prison guard was wearing for concealment-of-identity purposes.

"Yours?" I said, looking at the bike.

"Yeh," he said. "Brilliant, isn't it? She's a '60s Triumph, she is. You don't get many of those in good condition." There was pride in his voice when he said it. He stroked the thing as we went past.

"Painted red to match your hat?" I said.

"Yeh, helmet," he said. "Leo got me the helmet."

I was alive enough to notice that he'd left the keys sticking in the motorbike's ignition, which was no use to me then, given the condition I was in, but was certainly worth filing away for future use. Escape was very much on my mind, but I knew I had to take my time and figure out how to do it. I didn't fancy trying it on and having Leo catch me.

The room he led me into was a mess. There had been a stove in the corner, but it was rusty and half torn apart, the metal chimney lying on the floor with rust holes down the side. They had managed to light a small fire in it nevertheless, and the smoke was curling up through a hole in the roof where the pipe used to be. There was an old crate they sat me down on and some wooden boxes. Neatly folded against the wall on some newspapers were three sleeping bags. The window had been breeze-blocked at one time, but somebody had knocked out a few of the blocks to let in a little light.

Dodie, covered in her pillowcase, was sitting in a purple armchair, with gold braid around the sides and the springs sticking out of the arms. I still wonder how it ever got there. It was totally out of place. Leo was up against the wall, draped in his plastic shopping bag. The place badly needed some air. It smelled of burnt baked beans, which presumably had been their breakfast, cooked on the ruins of the broken stove.

The scene that followed was absolutely predictable. They must have seen the same hostage films I'd seen, or read the same books.

"We're worried about your mum, Suzie. How she's feeling and all," Dodie said. She was obviously to be their spokeswoman, which tied in with her being the one who had been giving me soup and cleaning me. My guess is that the two boys were uncomfortable about how to handle the situation when there was a girl in it. If I had been a boy, Leo might have tried rough stuff to get what he wanted, but Dodie had probably told him that she had more chance of persuading me with sweet talk.

"And I'm worried about freezing to death!" I said. "You can't leave me out there much longer in this cold."

I was concentrating on not letting them see how scared and weak I felt. I was still trembling with cold and feeling absolutely miserable, but I had keyed myself up to manage no quivers, no tears, head up, all that stuff. *Impossible stuff,* one part of me said. But I had to make it possible, because the only thing I had going for me was that I knew what I wanted: I wanted to get away from them, particularly Leo.

To do that, I had to keep my head and think straight.

"Nobody wants your mum worrying," Dodie went on coaxingly. "We thought you could write her a note. Just to say you were all right."

The two boys had moved in behind her, leaning against the wall. It was all very casual, but the hint of menace was very clear in their body language.

"She'll want to know you are all right,"

Dodie prompted when I didn't reply.

"If you want to stop my mum worrying, you should let me go," I managed, speaking slowly so that I could get the words out.

"You're kidding!" from Leo.

"You could tell your mum not to worry," Dodie said quickly.

Silence again when I made no reply. I could feel fear seeping through me. What would they do if I kept on saying no? It meant counting on the little Munchkin to keep Leo off me.

"Well?" from Leo.

"Let's get this straight," I said. "You want me to write a note to my mum, saying I'm all right? What else?"

I'd managed it. I don't know how I did, but my voice sounded firm, as if I knew what I was doing. I had to keep it that way.

"We'll tell you what to write," Gerard said through his helmet. I could see his eyes above the scarf, nothing else. It was very off-putting.

"I bet you would!" I said.

"She'll be desperate to hear from you," Dodie said. "Don't you want to make things easier for your mum?"

There was hesitation in her voice, which I took for a good sign. They'd been relying on me to cave in after my long period alone in the hut.

I think that is where they went wrong, really. Leaving me alone must have been

72

meant to break me, but in a funny way it worked in reverse. It was so bad, and I was so frightened, and cold and dirty and in pain, that something inside me hardened.

I knew that a note like that would put terrible pressure on my mum, and I wasn't going to let them use me to do that. Knowing I was alive wouldn't help her, because she would know how terrified I must be, and that would work on her mind and hurt her more than anything. Mum would feel she had to do something, but there was nothing she could do. She's not rich. She couldn't pay them. I thought I'd tell them that, straight out.

"There's no point in trying to terrorize my mum," I said, speaking very slowly so that they would take it in and believe me. "We haven't got any money."

"Your mum has a business," Leo said.

"That shop of your dad's. The tile shop on Main Street," Gerard said, nodding.

"In case you didn't know, my dad died years ago and the business has been sold. My mum is a teacher, and we are hanging on by the skin of our teeth, courtesy of the Northern Bank. There isn't going to be any big pay-off for letting me go."

"Don't believe you!" from Leo. "What money did you get for the shop?"

"Enough to pay off the bills Dad owed," I said.

I wished I could see Leo's face. A shopping bag is a shopping bag. You can't read much into the expression of a shopping bag.

"Don't believe you!" Leo repeated.

"That's your hard luck," I said. "I'm not writing any note."

"Suzie?" from Dodie doubtfully.

Leo started shouting at me.

I kept saying no, no way, because I wasn't going to put my family through the kind of fear I was going through.

Leo called me lots of names, and I was waiting for his rough stuff to start again, but he didn't try it.

It was really horrible crouching by the smoky stove in that dank little room with this big lad in his plastic shopping bag yelling at me.

You can only take so much. In the end, I started to cry.

"Stop it, Leo," I said. "I just won't write any note, and there isn't any way you can make me." I said something like that, anyway. It was chancing it a bit, I suppose – chancing that they weren't as ruthless as they were making out. If they had been really nasty, they could have made me do anything, because I have no illusions about my ability to stand up to pain. I was afraid of them but, even by then, I had sensed that they weren't real criminals. I clung to the conviction that they wouldn't really

74

hurt me if it came to it.

"She's had enough, Leo," urged Dodie – not before time!

"Shut up."

"Why don't you just let me go?" from me, on the floor, desperately. "This is silly. You think I know who you are, but I don't know any Leos, truly I don't. I can't think of a single Leo I know. So I don't know you."

It didn't convince Leo for a minute, but it was true enough. The name Leo meant nothing to me, and I'd been up and down the list of people I might be supposed to know, searching for a Leo. "You think I know you, but I don't," I insisted.

I was still insisting it when they stuck me back in the little goat hut at the side of the house.

"You going to write that note for us?" from Leo.

"No," from me.

"Then you can stay there till you rot!"

He slammed the door shut, leaving me alone again. The cold was very bad, even crouched over with the duvet to protect me. But being alone for so long in the darkness was worst of all.

There was nobody to see me when I was alone. I could give way – and I did – but after the sobbing and the shivering, nothing changed, and there I was. I had to start thinking again.

Leo believed I knew who he was.

He wasn't going to let me go.

I had to escape, or just stay where I was and wait for them to make up their stupid minds about what they intended to do with me, hoping that I wouldn't freeze to death first.

Their minds, all three – or just Leo's mind? At that stage, I didn't know or care which of them did the deciding, so long as they decided something and moved me out of that terrible place.

CHAPTER NINE

I love my mum very much.

That was why I'd refused to write their blackmailing note for them. If I had sent her the note they suggested, it would have half killed her. She'd have tried to raise the money for them somehow, tried to pay them off.

My three kidnappers hadn't meant to kidnap me. They weren't in the kidnapping-for-blood-money league. Having kidnapped me by accident, they tried to make me write a note, because that's what you do with a kidnapped person. But it didn't follow that they would either chop bits off me or send me home in return for a briefcase full of marked notes left under a bush.

Unless I could come up with an escape plan that looked like it would work, the best I could do was to keep talking and hope that they wouldn't harm me.

Meanwhile, I was making the headlines in a way Mum and Ruth could well have done without.

HUNT FOR SUZIE Q, 15. MOTHER'S PLEA: RELEASE MY CHILD.

They all had that kind of thing, despite the fact that none of the newspaper reporters had heard so much as a word from my family, thanks to the good offices of the police and Alan Flynn from down the lane.

I saw the clippings afterwards in the hospital. They had used a really awful photo, one taken with Simon and Woodsy when we were at the Don't Close Our Hospitals demonstration. They cut Simon and Woodsy out of it, and there I was in this gross outfit that made me look about thirteen and absolutely and completely weird.

HAVE YOU SEEN SUZIE? was all over the *Daily Mirror*.

Why, during the one time in my life when I was famous-for-a-day-Suzie, did the picture have to be of me jumping around with a stupid felt hat on my head, a pair of bell-bottom pants that came out of Noah's Ark, and Ruth's cat's eye glasses propped up on my forehead? The bell-bottoms had red and purple roses up the legs. They were Mum's old ones from her flower power days in the Sixties. Ruth and I had decided to go the demo looking like Sixties clones, much to Mum's amusement. It is the only time in my life that I've dressed like that but, as far as the world knows now, that's Suzie Q, the Councillor's daughter who was kidnapped and held hostage. If I ever have kids, I'll have no chance of convincing them that their mum wasn't an absolute banana when she was fifteen.

Mum and Ruth had a terrible time keeping the papers away from Davie. They managed the TV by telling him it was broken and the man would be coming to fix it, and they hid all the radios in Mum's bedroom, where they could listen to them secretly and report to each other. But he knew quite well that something was up.

Ruth says the birthday party was a real experience, set against the backdrop of TV and radio reports saying I was dead in the lake, or words hinting at that anyway, and police and reporters jostling in our lane.

"How can we have a party with all this going on?" Ruth asked.

"We're having it, whatever! I don't believe that Suzie is dead, and she would want him to have his party," Mum said.

In desperation Ruth suggested that they get Mrs Flynn down the lane to have Davie's party in her house, but Mum was absolutely dead set against it, even though Mrs Flynn was more than willing. Ruth says Mrs Flynn was really good. She told Alan to block the lane with their tractor and trailer so the newspapermen couldn't get up to worry us.

The newspapermen were obscene!

You have to picture the way it was. There was every reason to believe that I was lying somewhere on the bottom of Passenger's Lake, with a brick tied around my neck to stop me from bobbing up. The police were not saying so, but all their actions showed it: boats out on the lake, frogmen being called in. Naturally, the first thing Ruth thought of was that they would be taken to the lake.

"No!" from our tame policewoman.

"Why not?" defiantly from Ruth.

Margaret pointed out that the lane up to our house, as far as the tractor, was thick with men and cameras. If they tried to leave the house, the little men would follow. There'd be a cross-country hunt, with Mum and Ruth as the foxes.

The perfect newspaper photo apparently: MOTHER BY THE LAKESIDE, WHILE THE FROGMEN ARE OUT FISHING FOR HER DAUGHTER.

"I don't think your mother would like that, Ruth," said Margaret tactfully.

"But we must go!" Ruth was in tears.

"No," from my mum decisively.

"Mum... " from Ruth.

"Suzie isn't there," from Mum.

Mum kept on saying it, and that rather put an end to Ruth's protests. Mum doesn't know why she was so sure that I wasn't in the lake, that I was still alive. Some animal thing inside her, she says. Ruth didn't feel that way; she was convinced I was dead, and enraged that they were being kept prisoners in their house, not able to do anything about looking for me.

"Can't you stop them, send them away?" she said to Margaret.

"It's very difficult," Margaret said. "So far they aren't doing anything illegal. It is a public place. They have every right to be there."

Luckily not everyone shared that opinion.

Mrs Flynn's son Alan, for a start. Alan is a harmless big soul, but he has a thing about trespass on his mother's land. Apparently two men in a car had driven into Flynn's field, which lies across the back of our house, and were busy with a pair of wirecutters at our back garden fence. Alan, working in the barn, saw them at it. He grabbed his shotgun and ran up the field, yelling at the men.

They told him where he could go, in no uncertain terms, which is a dangerous thing to do with someone as simple and uncomplicated as Alan.

Bang! Bang! Alan let their windsreen have it, both barrels.

He says they were off like rabbits – with him yelling and shouting behind them – abandoning their wirecutters and some fancy leather gardening gloves but, true to Press traditions, clutching their precious cameras.

That led to Alan being arrested by the police, Mrs Flynn arriving at our house, and Mum being physically prevented by police-woman Margaret from intervening. It was all smoothed over somehow, with Mum weighing in to point out that it wasn't just trespass, because they had been in the act of damaging our fence with their wirecutters. In the end the police closed the road just outside Cloughanny to all but the few locals who live out our way.

That didn't stop reporters from coming on foot, behind the hedges. Despite the closed road, Mum and Ruth were kept in a state of siege all day, and there wasn't anything they could do about it.

Our policewoman also coped with the incoming mail. She set up office in our kitchen, opening Davie's birthday cards and the bills. There were a few letters she wouldn't let Ruth see. Ruth thinks they were obscene ones from weirdos.

I'm very surprised that Mum let her do that. Ruth says Mum was very rational about it. Ms Margaret Campbell told her that they wanted to do it and she said, "Yes, go ahead." Mum says that she believed the police would do it anyway, and she felt sure it was better to co-operate with them than to try to fight.

Once young Alan Flynn had shown them it was necessary to teach the rotten reporters a lesson, the police seemed to take a much more active approach to the photographers and gawkers. There were wild episodes with the police chasing photographers out of the bushes behind our barn. One of them climbed a tree, and the police took his ladder and left him up there until he gave them his film. I don't think what the police did can have been strictly legal, but it certainly worked. Ruth and Mum both agree that without them the whole thing would have been impossible – not that it wasn't impossible enough already.

Then, in the middle of the whole commotion, Ruth and Mum found themselves coping with the party: half a dozen of Davie's school friends, complete with paper hats, together with their doting mothers. Normally the mums would have dumped them and run, but not this time. Having fought their way through the media men to get to our door, the neighbours stayed on to sympathize with Mum and Ruth, to organize the party games, and to complain about the reporters.

Ruth says it was a total nightmare.

Somebody said something to Davie, of course. Mum had prepared him, half explaining what had happened, but his little school friends must have been more direct.

He came out with it after the party was over and the last of the visiting mums had cleared off.

"Why did the bad men take our Suzie?" he asked Ruth.

Ruth said they were silly men.

"When is Suzie Q coming back?"

Ruth said she didn't know.

"Will the bad men come here?"

"Why is that police lady here?"

"Will the bad men hurt Suzie Q?"

"I want our Suzie Q."

It was about half-past nine before they could get him to bed. It must have been just about then that I attacked Leo with the roof beam.

The idea was to brain him, but it didn't work out exactly as planned.

CHAPTER TEN

Attacking Leo wasn't smart, but I'd been working on the idea of escape, and when a chance suddenly presented itself, I suppose I had a rush of blood to the head. I didn't stop to think how impossible it was.

I wasn't as cold as before, because Dodie had come up with another old duvet and two blankets to wrap around me, but I still felt pretty miserable, lying tied up in the goat hut. The cobbled floor was dank, and the only light was through the rusty holes in the old tin roof. Even that went at dusk.

I filled in the time as best I could with the escape problem. So long as I remained tied up, there clearly wasn't a hope. But if I could get my hands untied and the ankle rope off, the impossible process of digging my way out through the cobbled floor, scraping stones out of the wall with my bare hands, or beating down the padlocked door could commence!

The process wasn't as impossible as it seemed anyway. I'd already worked that out, because stone walls and stone floors and a locked door do not a prison make, if you have your wits about you and use your eyes – and I'd had plenty of time to do that.

Getting the ropes off my wrists was the initial sticking point. In books and films any old heroine worth her salt can do that without a blink. I couldn't. My hands remained securely tied, despite all my efforts to wear the rope out by rubbing my wrists against sharp stone edges. The result was bleeding wrists and chafed skin, not instant freedom.

It was a long time before they bothered to come near me again, long after nightfall. Then Dodie appeared with a flashlight, presumably to check out that I hadn't expired. I was ready for her. Act bright and tough, show no despair; take her face on was the approach I thought would work best. Dodie plainly wasn't happy about what was going on. Neither was I, but I thought acting confident and on top of the game might work to my advantage.

"What happened to you?" she said in a none too friendly voice, shining the light in my face.

"I nearly killed myself trying to get these ropes off my wrists," I said, because even she was bound to catch on that that was what I had been doing. She only had to look at my raw and bleeding skin to guess what I'd been up to.

"You should have left well enough alone," she said.

"Have you any idea what it's like?" I said. "Listen, this place is freezing. I am tied up and very cold, and if you leave me here like this much longer, you'll have a corpse on your hands, and that won't solve anything, will it?"

"I'm freezing, too," she said.

"You can move about," I told her. "I'm stuck in this position. All I can do is roll over. You'll damage my circulation and my hands will fall off. You need to untie me."

Direct and to the point, and note the attempt to sound cheerful and upbeat in adversity. I could have curled up and moaned on the floor and acted as though I was dying, but my instinct was that that wouldn't work with her. I was feeling very bad physically, suffering from a combination of cold and cramp, but I was determined not to let her see how weak I really was.

"Yeh," she said, looking down at me on the floor. "So you can get away!"

"It's got nothing to do with getting away," I said. "How could I get out of here, even if my hands were free? I can't break down the door, and I'm hardly likely to be able to dig through the floor with my fingernails, am I? I could bang my head against the wall, but it would take a long time to dislodge big stone blocks, don't you think?"

"Nobody could," she agreed, flicking the flashlight beam around the walls. The wetness running down them glistened in the beam.

"So you don't *need* to keep me tied up," I said. "You really don't. It is cruel and unnecessary, and if I ever get out of this, I'm going to say so. It would be different if I had any chance of escape, but I haven't. You can see that, even if the others can't."

"Yeh," she said. "You're right."

"Then help me a bit," I said. "You may need me, you know. If you get caught, you'll want me saying nice things. Not that you tortured me ... and that is what this is, because the ropes are really hurting and my wrists are all swollen up and I am freezing to death."

"Leo said we had to keep you tied," she said doubtfully.

"I know that," I told her. "You are scared of him and I can understand that too. That is what I would tell the cops and my mum. This is really all Leo's fault. Then the cops are going to ask, 'Well, how did they treat you?' and I am going to have to say nobody did anything at all to help me. And that isn't going to sound good, is it?"

"I can't do nothing," she said.

"Yes, you can," I said. "You can untie my wrists."

"Leo would know," she said.

Plainly Leo knowing was a fate worse than death, and she wasn't going to risk that, so I went for second best.

"You could slack off the rope around my wrists, so that I can keep my circulation going and move a bit, but you don't need to untie me completely. You leave it so that if Leo comes, I can tighten them. Then Leo will never know. All you have to do is make a noise so I know Leo is about to come, right?"

"Y–e–s," she said. "Only… "

"Only what?" I said.

"If you got out, Leo would know it was me," she said.

"I can't get out!" I said. "I can't scrape my way through these walls, can I? I won't try anything, honestly. I am not that stupid."

It should have been obvious to anyone with an ounce of wit that I was lying, and had no intention of keeping my word. I have never been a particularly good liar, so I don't really know how I managed it.

Somewhat reluctantly, she loosened the rope.

"That's great," I said, though it didn't feel one bit great. I was biting my lips to hold back the pain as the blood started moving again through the bruised veins.

"Good," she said.

"What about some food? I'm really starving."

"We've got cans," she said. "Baked beans and stuff."

"Baked beans would be great," I said.

She went off to get them, taking the flashlight with her, and carefully padlocking the door.

Find the beans, find the can opener, heat them up … I had about ten minutes. I could see the chance of doing something for the first time, and I decided to go for it – which was plain crazy, in the circumstances.

Ropes off, that was the first thing. That didn't take me long.

It shows how desperate I was that I had no doubt at all about what I was going to do. When she came back and undid the padlock again, she'd be carrying the beans and the flashlight, which meant she would be in no position to defend herself. The door opened inwards. When she came through the door, I would be positioned, out of sight, ready to attack her, using the remains of one of the rotten old roof timbers as a club to beat her brains out with.

Bang her on the head, knock her cold, straight out and over to Gerard's bike, with the keys in the ignition. Off down the road.

I was so scared and so angry that I didn't stop to calculate the risk of not bringing it off, even though I've never even sat on a motorbike, let alone started or ridden one.

I got myself up against the wall, beside the door, when I heard her coming. I reasoned that she would come through the door, ducking her head, so she would have her neck bent and exposed. I would bash her one on the back of the neck and floor her. I wasn't worried about hurting her, maybe even injuring her for life. In my book she had asked for it.

Unfortunately it was not Dodie but Leo, still wearing his shopping bag, who came with the baked beans.

I hit him as hard as I could, but the beam was so rotten that it disintegrated on impact in a shower of dust and woodlice and baked beans, and the next moment, he had me pinned against the wall and was pummelling me with both fists.

"You stupid cow!" he shouted, and he sent me sprawling on the floor on top of the baked beans and tomato sauce which were supposed to be my supper.

"You're not getting away as easily as that," he said, picking up his flashlight from the floor.

Then he lifted up the plate he'd dropped, amazingly unshattered, which still had more than half the baked beans on it – the half I wasn't lying on.

Very slowly and deliberately, he upended the plate of beans over my head.

"Enjoy your supper, Suzie Q!" he said.

He left me bean-covered and weeping on the floor. He didn't even bother to tie me up. I'm sure he thought that by then he had done enough to convince me that escaping wasn't on.

He was right about that. The not very subtle beans-over-my-head touch made the point that I couldn't take them on physically. I'd have to concentrate on talking my way out of trouble.

CHAPTER ELEVEN

I wasn't sure what to expect from Dodie when she came the following morning, considering what Leo must have told her. I didn't think I would be her favourite person, now that she knew I'd been intending to brain her.

She turned up bright, matter-of-fact, but not over-friendly, which was as good as I could expect. If somebody had tried to brain me, I'd have been a lot more upset than she seemed to me, but then maybe her world contained more routine violence than mine did.

"Leo says you're not to try that again," she warned me. "He says you know what you'll get if you do. And there is no use trying it anyway, because you couldn't get away from here."

"Right," I said. "I hope you didn't get into trouble with Leo?"

"Oh, he's all pleased, 'cause you made me

look silly," she said, without rancour. Then she added, "He smelled a rat. That's why he had the beans off me and delivered them himself. You were lucky he didn't hurt you!"

"I suppose I was," I said.

"I've brought you some food," she said, and she put the baked beans plate down on the floor. "Try eating it this time, instead of rolling in it."

My clothes still bore signs of the baked bean battle.

"I'll turn into a baked bean soon!" I said ruefully.

"I know the feeling too well!" she said. "I'm sick of them. But in my condition I've got to eat, haven't I? And there isn't anything else."

In my condition...?

That was when I got it ... the sum of various things she'd let slip and her Munchkin appearance. I didn't say anything. I lay there, pretending I was half dead, on my last legs, with my mind whirring away. I was sure I was right ... but how could I use it, if at all?

"You won't be running anywhere today, will you?" she said, almost teasingly.

"I don't think I'm fit to run, even if I could get out of here," I said, playing up to her.

She put her hand under my arms and pulled me into a kneeling position. I let her do it. I sat there with my head down, trying to get across the message that I'd accepted my lot and wasn't going to try anything.

"Come on," she said. "It's not that bad. Nobody is going to hurt you."

"Then why don't you let me go?" I muttered.

It was impossible to tell if there was any reaction, because of the pillowcase covering her head and face.

I looked at her carefully, the pillowcase to her shoulders and her fat little body swelled out below. It had been obvious all along, and I just hadn't caught on. I suppose I had my mind on other things. All that stuff about me not knowing how messed up her life was … I was right! I knew I was right!

Time to launch a Munchkin offensive, just to see where it would get me. If nothing else, it would keep her talking and, if I could do that, I might be able to work some advantage out of it. I was hoping I could get our relationship back on a girls-together footing.

Direct attack, I thought. Take her off guard.

"When's your baby due?" I asked.

"I'm twenty-two weeks," she said in a surprised voice.

Got you! I thought. It had hardly been more than a hunch, but it looked like it would pay off.

"It's Gerard's," she said.

"I hope he's not leaving you as a single mother, then," I said.

"We're married," she said. "Gerard was really good about it. I'm Dodie Rice now, me!" She sounded really proud and pleased. She'd given me their second name, *Rice*. Gerard and Dodie *Rice*. She was off-guard, but even so, she might have tried a bit harder. I suppose her mind was only on one thing just then.

He should be good about it, considering he's the one who got you pregnant, I thought. She couldn't have been more than sixteen. I thought he must be a little older, and it turned out later that I was right.

"Only Gerard can't get work," she went on.

Her psychology was truly amazing! The night before, I had set out to brain her and dump her in my hut, while I made my escape. In her place I'd have kept my guard up for ever more after a thing like that, but it didn't seem to faze her. I can only think that she was almost as scared and tense as I was, and that talking to me eased the strain.

It all gushed out of her. She was pregnant, he was out of work, with no qualifications, and they had no money and no prospects. There is little work around our bit of the country, even if you have a string of diplomas, so I wasn't exactly surprised. She talked about how they were going to move on and Gerard was going to find work and they would get a council house or a flat somewhere and everything would be hunky-dory in the best of all possible worlds.

"It's just the cops," she said. "If the cops left Gerard alone, we would be all right."

I almost choked on my baked beans! There didn't seem to be any connection in her mind between her Gerard's actions and the police showing an interest in him. Robbing supermarkets for a start, and holding people prisoner against their will; it sounded to me like the kind of behaviour pattern that might just lead to the police taking an interest.

"If they get him this time, he'll go to prison," she said earnestly. "I don't know why they keep picking on him."

This time. Prison. Blunt, just like that. Then I realized she would go to prison as well. She'd have her baby in prison.

Then she said an astonishing thing, out of the blue.

"We were on the radio news," she said. "Our names and all! Not just yours." Which seemed to explain the thing about telling me their names. Keeping their full names secret wasn't important anymore.

It wasn't what she said that was astonishing; it didn't take much intelligence to guess that we would be news. It was the way she said it that was so weird. She was proud that their names had been read out on the radio.

"If the police know your names, then there is absolutely no point in walking around with a pillowcase on your head for my benefit, is there?"

"Yeh," she said doubtfully.

"It doesn't matter whether I know who Leo is now or not!" I burst out. "Can't you see? If the police know who you are already, to the point when they are putting your names out on the news, whether or not I can identify you isn't going to make any difference to anyone!"

It also meant they didn't need to keep me anymore. There was no point. Something had happened; they'd been identified by witnesses or someone had given their names to the police. I was no longer the chief witness for the prosecution!

"Leo said to keep it on," she said.

"Well, Leo is a bloody loony then!" I said.

"Leo's name wasn't on the news," she said. "Only Gerard and me. And Leo says they might have our names but they still have to prove it, and you would be a witness, wouldn't you?"

I took that in. Just my luck that Leo hadn't been identified … but surely he would be able to work out that with the other two named on the radio, his involvement was bound to surface.

"I'd be a witness if I have to be," I said. "But I could tell them it *wasn't* you, couldn't I?"

The moment I'd said it, I knew it was a mistake.

"I'm not falling for that one!" she said.

"I could tell them you didn't mean it all to happen," I amended, trying to retrieve the situation.

"Yeh," she said, not sounding as if she believed me for a minute.

"It is true, though," I said. "You didn't mean it to happen this way, did you? That's why I don't want you to go sending little notes to my mum. It wouldn't be just for abducting me you'd be in for, but kidnapping for ransom, which is much worse. If I let you do that, then nothing I could say would help you, would it? You'd definitely all go to prison."

"Leo says we won't," she said defiantly.

"It strikes me that Leo got you into this mess," I said. "I wouldn't go by what Leo has to say, if I were you."

Silence.

"Why don't you talk to Gerard about it?" I said. "He won't want you having your baby in prison, will he? That's what's going to happen if this all goes wrong."

"Gerard's all upset," she said. "Leo only got into this to help us, because me and Gerard were stuck with the baby coming, like. Now Gerard is all upset at the way it has turned out."

"So he should be!" I said bitterly.

"They never done anything like this before, Leo and my Gerard," she said. "It was just me

99

being pregnant and all, and no money and no job. And Leo said it would be all right." This speech didn't tie in with the "he'll go to prison this time". Probably her Gerard had a record for teenage joy-riding, or pinching cigarettes, but I let it pass, because I had more important things to do than check out his character references.

"It needn't be that bad," I said, trying to be positive. "Maybe my mum could help him. She knows a lot of people, with her Council work."

"Does she?" Dodie asked, hopeful suddenly.

I felt mean. I knew that if Mum could lay her hands on the Munchkin's precious Gerard, she would probably tear him limb from limb after what had happened to me.

"I'm sure she would try," I said, easily forgiving myself for the lie.

"He done a Youth Training Scheme," she said. "Plumbing. With McGovern and McIvor. They were all right, only they had no job for him."

Joe McGovern used the scheme for cheap labour. He isn't the only one, of course. That is just the way life works around here. You can't blame Joe McGovern. It is a two-man firm, one Protestant and one Catholic, so they can get jobs from both sides. They have been driving around together in their little van for years. It is a partnership, and they were highly unlikely to take her Gerard in as a third man, particularly if they heard that he'd been in trouble with the police.

"My mum knows a lot of plumbers," I said, somewhat helplessly.

Another silence, while she thought about it.

"Only we're in this mess, now, aren't we?" She broke out of her thoughts with a vengeance, daylight dawning. "We didn't plan all this to happen. It just *has*, you know. We were just after some money."

I didn't say anything. I let her stew in it.

"It's going to be all right," she said. "Leo will think of something. He'll get Gerard and me out some way. He won't let nothing happen to us."

"Well, I hope he does think of something for all our sakes!" I said. "But if he doesn't, I promise I'll ask Mum to help you and Gerard. I really will. And if there's a job going at the plumbing, I'll ask her to help you."

I suppose you have to be a blind optimist if you have a boyfriend whose name is Gerard and you let him go around wearing a helmet with BIG G on it to *conceal* his identity, but I didn't think for a moment that she would take the plumbing bit seriously.

CHAPTER TWELVE

The possible threat posed by Leo "coming up" with something that would save their bacon occupied my mind for the next half hour or so. Maybe he would cut one of my ears off and send it through the mail? What was I going to do if he started working on some crazed solution to their problems like that? I was still thinking about it when Dodie turned up again.

"Hi, Suzie Q," she said affably. "Gerard's come to see you about the plumbing!"

No pillowcase on Dodie, no racing helmet and scarf concealing Gerard's beauty! Evidently I had made a social breakthrough.

There was an awkward pause while they stood looking at me, and I sat taking in the totally unexpected view!

Gerard looked a bit older than the Munchkin. He had the same old jeans and trainers on that he'd worn at the time of the robbery, and a loose green sweater with stains down the front. The edge of a tattoo, showing at his wrist, proclaimed his love for his mother.

The Munchkin, minus her pillowcase, wasn't very prepossessing either. She had a little fat face that could have been pretty, if you go for the doll type, but wasn't helped by the shaggy haircut that petered out around her ears. The Liverpool shirt she was wearing, complete with sponsor's logo, stretched uncomfortably over her twenty-two-week-pregnant bump. She looked tired and worn, underneath a kind of forced buoyancy. Both of them had the same dull complexion, a poor diet look.

This *is* how they looked. The government can say all it likes about a classless society, but some people have the money to buy proper food and clothes and other people haven't, and it shows.

"Gerard wants to talk to you about the plumbing," Dodie prompted, doing her best to wink at me optimistically.

There was a brief pause while I adjusted my mind and she smiled anxiously at me, and then hopefully at Gerard.

So be it. We were in for a cosy chat about Gerard's career prospects.

"About your mum," Dodie said, prompting me again. "About your mum maybe getting Gerard a job at the plumbing?"

She was all bright-eyed and hopeful, anticipating that she had pulled a stroke that was going to change their lives. Meanwhile, my mind was in mid-boggle.

"That's right," said Gerard. "I done plumbing."

"Well, OK," I said, thinking frantically. "Let's talk. I mean, I'd like to be able to help you, if I can. But I would like to talk in the open air." The truth of it was that I was desperate to be out of the hut. I'd been in there for far too long. It was small, smelly, and dank, all damp stone floor and rusty tin roof on decaying timbers. I needed to breathe.

Gerard looked doubtful.

"She won't try anything, Gerard," the Munchkin put in. "She knows better now."

"Honest!" I said dishonestly, but there was no point in worrying about my immortal soul. I had to get everything I could out of a real no-win situation.

"Well, all right," Gerard said.

They brought me out of the hut, and we sat on the boulders outside. It was bitterly cold, but I put that behind me and rejoiced in the blessed relief of seeing sunlight again, and being able to breathe fresh air.

"Does that feel better?" Dodie asked.

"Oh, yes," I said, looking around me. "Lovely. I mean it's really nice up here, isn't it? Beautiful view."

It sounded babbling crazy, if you ask me! Meanwhile, my mind was going at a rate of knots, trying to work out the best way to play the situation.

Dodie looked pleased, presumably operating on the theory that she had done me a favour, and now I would be able to do one for her Gerard, in return.

"Tell her, Gerard," Dodie said, nudging him.

"I done plumbing," Gerard repeated earnestly.

"Mr McGovern said he was really good," Dodie put in proudly. "Gerard would have been kept on, only there wasn't enough work."

"I see," I said.

"And you said your mum knew some plumbers," Dodie ploughed on, obviously anxious that I would confirm what she had told Gerard. The incredible thing was that he had fallen for it.

"Yes. Well, she does," I said. "Mum knows lots of plumbers."

"I'm a good worker," Gerard said. "I was never off sick once."

What did they expect me to say? My mind was running around in circles. Talk about getting Gerard a job had just been words, a desperate try to worm something, anything, out of the Munchkin. I'd never expected her to take it at face value and go running off to tell him about a job opportunity. For the life of me I couldn't grasp how they could believe that kidnapping me and keeping me in a freezing cold mountain hut could somehow lead to a job opportunity for Gerard.

"Do you think your mum would help us?" Dodie said.

What really cut through me was the hope in her voice. How could I sit there and lie to her … well, easily enough, as it turned out!

"I'm sure she would try, if I asked her," I said lamely.

"What plumbers does she know?" Gerard asked, narrowing his eyes, to let me see he wasn't anybody's fool.

I reeled off all the plumbers I could remember. McAllisters. Arthur Wright. The Beanstalk McCarthy.

"Beanstalk wouldn't have me," he said. "We wrecked one of his generators once. Me and Leo. For a laugh." He smiled, remembering it.

"That was Leo, not you," the Munchkin said hastily.

"The cops got on to us," Gerard added. "Leo only did it because the Beanstalk was mouthing me. I couldn't answer back because I was hoping he'd put me on full-time, so Leo wrecked his generator. Only I got blamed, so I don't think Beanstalk would take me on now."

"Yes, well, there are others," I said, and I invented a few, rapidly expanding Mum's role of local Councillor from the provision of dust-bins and burial grounds to include being the power behind all local contracting decisions.

"Does she know any plumbers in Scotland?" Dodie asked earnestly. "We were thinking we might go over there."

"Because of all this trouble we're in," Gerard explained. "We could make a new start, and the cops wouldn't bother us there, would they? Like they wouldn't know who I was, so they wouldn't come bothering me."

"Maybe some of the plumbers Mum knows would have friends in Scotland," I said.

"Would your mum do it, though?" Dodie broke in.

"Well, she might," I said, lying through my teeth. "But we'll have to sort this end of things out first, won't we? I mean, she's not going to help you get a job with me like this, is she?"

Pregnant pause.

"If we let you go, you'd talk to her?" Dodie asked.

"I would, yes."

I knew I was lying; it wasn't true. It felt like a Judas act, taking advantage of two kids who were in an absolutely helpless situation by offering them hope when there wasn't any, and I knew for sure there wasn't. There wasn't going to be any plumbing job for Gerard that

107

would lead to having a nice little Scottish lochside home with haggis on the table for tea. How could I play on their weaknesses like that?

"You're very good," Dodie said warmly, making me feel even worse.

Gerard was looking worried again.

"It isn't just us, though," he said. "It's down to Leo, too, isn't it? Leo's in it, too. And he got in it trying to help us out, so I'm not dumping Leo."

There was a touch of defiance in his voice, directed not so much at me as at Dodie.

"Leo's been awfully good to us," Dodie put in, as much for Gerard's benefit as mine. She didn't sound that convinced about it all the time.

I doubted my powers of Leo-persuasion, so I tried to head that one off.

"I don't think you two owe Leo anything," I said, implying that I believed they were almost innocent, and Leo was responsible for all my ills. I thought that they would want me to see it that way, since I was supposed to make Gerard's case to Mum. "Leo doesn't need to be involved."

"There's no way I'm going to cross Leo," Gerard said firmly. "Leo's my mate. We look after each other."

"He does try his best to help you, but he gets you in trouble too, Gerard," Dodie said, not very persuasively. "Like over your bike. Taking those parts. You nearly lost your bike over Leo."

"If it wasn't for Leo, I wouldn't have no bike," Gerard said. "Leo's my best mate. I'm not dumping Leo. No way!"

"Gerard...?" Dodie started bitterly.

"You come," he said, speaking to me. "See if you can talk Leo around."

I don't suppose I've done anything meaner in my life than half persuading them that my mum could fix Gerard up with a job in Scotland, and I suppose being taken to tell Leo about it served me right!

We headed for the house, ducking our heads beneath the low door frame to enter the same bare room I'd been in before. The only addition to it was a map lying on the floor, and a toasting fork beside the smouldering fire in the little stove.

"Leo?" Gerard called.

"What the hell!" A door at the side opened, and then shut again quickly.

"Get her out!" angrily, through the closed door.

"It's OK, Leo!" Dodie said.

"There's no way she's seeing my face!" Leo growled.

"Ease up, Leo!" Gerard said.

Then the door opened, and Leo came slouching through it.

He'd put on his plastic shopping bag.

"Don't be daft, Leo!" Dodie said. "Take it off."

The shopping bag hovered menacingly, keeping close to the wall of the room away from me.

"You don't need that thing," I said. I had a notion that going head on at him and making him look silly might help me. "You are the one I'm supposed to know from way back, after all!"

"Maybe you don't remember me," he said, sounding sullen and defensive. "You *ought* to know me, though. Know me enough to be able to recognize me if you saw me, that is."

At least he'd given some ground.

"If you thought of that to begin with, I wouldn't be here!" I said bitterly.

"I'm still certain you know me," he said, taking back the ground he'd just given away.

"If I do, then you don't need the shopping bag!"

"I'm keeping it on. You're not seeing my face!" he said, illogical and belligerent at the same time, and plainly very confused.

"I don't want to," I said.

There was a long silence. I was waiting for Dodie or Gerard to break the good news that I was big in the Scottish plumbing world, via my mum's position of special influence. They seemed to have much less difficulty in believing it than I had, and I thought they might do it better than I would.

"Well?" he said suspiciously. "What's this all about?"

Skip the plumbing job line, I decided regretfully. There was no way I was going to persuade Leo that Councillor Mrs Quinn would look after them all.

Let the straight-talking commence!

"Look," I said. "You are in a mess, all three of you. You know that and I know that. I'm in it too, because you've dragged me in it. I want out."

"You're not putting anything over on me," Leo said suspiciously. "I'm not stupid like some people."

The Munchkin looked as if she was going to intervene, but then she didn't. Gerard had faded into the background, as before. Why hadn't he the guts to stand up for himself? I was beginning to lose patience with Gerard.

"Right, Leo. You're not stupid," I said, deciding to go for broke. "So you must know you are all going to be caught. There's no way you are going to get away with this. And if you hurt me or do anything to me, it is going to be much worse when you are caught. What you need is me on your side, and my mum. My mum has a lot of clout with the cops. She can talk to them. I'll explain—"

"That's crap, too!" he said.

"Her mum knows people in plumbing," the hapless Dodie chose to put in at that point. "Her mum could get you a job, Leo ... and Gerard. You and Gerard, Leo. In Scotland or some place where the cops don't know you."

"Get us put away inside for a long time, more like," Leo said.

There was a long silence.

"Well?" he said to me. "That's true, isn't it, Suzie Q?"

"Not necessarily," I said. "Not if ... if ... if we could work out some story between us. How you treated me well and everything. I'd put in a word, and Mum would and – "

It was obviously no use.

"You're probably right," I said, giving up the ghost. "You'll all go to prison for a very long time when you are caught."

The Munchkin gave a little yelp of distress behind me.

"You know it, and I know it," I said. "But you've got to come out again, haven't you? Then my mum *might* help you. I mean, she *really* could, if she wanted to. She knows a lot of people. And if she put in a word, you might not get such a long sentence. If you did some course or something inside, whatever you like, Mum could help you get a job doing it outside."

"Crap!" from Leo again.

He was right, of course. It was. Once he'd

said it, the Munchkin and her mate must have realized it too. I could feel them turning against me.

"It's time I told you how it is," Leo said.

"Leo—" from Dodie.

"You've said enough!" he snapped.

Then he came toward me and grabbed me by the arm.

"We're going for a walk, Suzie Q," he said.

"Don't you hurt her, Leo," came anxiously from Dodie, and a mutter of dissent from Gerard, although he didn't move. I couldn't count on Gerard for anything it seemed. His Munchkin was the one with the guts.

Leo bundled me through the door.

We were out in the cold air and I was absolutely terrified, with no idea of what was coming next. I kept thinking I had to keep cool and not let him reach me, but I was so scared that it must have showed.

"This-a-way," he said, and he pushed me so that I stumbled.

We were going away from the house, towards the face of the quarry.

"I thought you knew the score after your baked beans. Now I see I'm going to have to spell it out for you again," he said.

We'd come up on top of a rock, and beneath us there was a wide pool of stagnant water, with two oil drums floating on the greasy surface.

I was scared. I thought he was going to chuck me into the pool. It was then I said something I'm really ashamed of.

"Please let me go," I said. "Please Leo, let me go home."

It was stupid. He wasn't going to let me go home, and I should never have let myself get so low that I could plead with him, but I did, and I feel bad about it.

He picked up a stone from the ground and tossed it into the air.

It fell with a loud plop.

"That's deep, that is," Leo said. "Nobody knows how deep."

"Yes," I said.

"If you were in there with a stone tied around your neck, nobody would ever find you," he said. "That would be one way of solving our problem, wouldn't it?"

"You don't mean that," I said. "You can't mean that. You don't know what you are saying."

"Oh, but I do," he said.

"Dodie promised me—" I started to say.

The next moment his hand came out from beneath the shopping bag.

It was holding a gun, which he pointed straight at me, pressing the barrel hard into my neck, just beneath the jawline.

I went absolutely cold, quivering and cowering inside. I'm not ashamed of that – how

114

would anyone react with a gun pressed against their neck? People say a gun was used during the robbery itself, but I hadn't seen it up until then. It came as a terrible shock.

"You can twist them two all you like," Leo said. "But you're not twisting me, Suzie Q. And saying please and thank you in the right places isn't going to make any difference."

I nodded.

"You needn't think anybody is going to come and get you, because if they do turn up, they'll need skin divers to fish you out of that pool. Right?"

I believed what he was saying to me. If the police did turn up, then he would put the gun to my head and ask them what they intended doing about it. If no one turned up, they would eventually make their move, and what happened to me then wasn't going to depend on silly little Dodie, or her hapless Gerard.

My life depended on Leo, and his gun.

CHAPTER THIRTEEN

If I was scared stiff up at the quarry pool, Ruth and Mum weren't having it easy either.

The truth is that you can't go searching lakes for dead bodies without the word getting out. The police tried to be discreet, but of course the papers and TV got hold of it, and that in turn built up the tension in the house. Mum was convinced that I was alive, but Ruth wasn't. Ruth thought I was at the bottom of the lake.

Ruth came downstairs looking grim, determined that she was going to the lake, even if Mum wasn't.

"Suzie is my sister," she told Ms Margaret Campbell fiercely.

The policewoman tried to convince her that watching the frogmen at Passenger's Lake was the last thing she should be doing, but Ruth would have none of it. This time Mum backed her up, because she could see that Ruth needed to do something.

"Well, if you both really want to go, I'll fix a car," Margaret said.

"We'll go in our own car," Mum said.

"There are at least a dozen reporters and three TV crews down the road at the bottom of your lane, Mrs Quinn," Margaret pointed out. "If you drive down there and make for Plumber's Point, you'll have the whole lot of them in a convoy on your tail, plus the ones who are shopping around town for stories about Suzie. I don't think you would like that, would you?"

"I don't care!" Mum said.

"I think you would, when you saw the pictures they would print next day. They have a job to do and you'd be offering them a photo opportunity they couldn't afford to miss."

"We could put blankets over our heads or something," Ruth suggested, thinking of the way people are taken into courthouses. "You see it all the time on TV."

"How can I drive with a blanket over my head?" Mum snapped.

"They'd know our car anyway," Ruth added.

"I don't think you should go to the lake," Margaret said.

"No harm to you, but we're going!" Mum replied firmly, growing more determined by

117

the minute. If Ruth needed to go, they were going. That was it, as far as Mum was concerned.

"Then the question is, how do we get you there without bringing a pack of photographers on your tail?"

It was Mum who came up with the answer, as usual.

Alan Flynn again.

She decided she would take advantage of the Flynns' good neighbour offer, and use them and their car. It was no use trying to nip across the fields in daylight, because they would have undoubtedly been spotted, so Mum phoned and arranged for Alan to drive his mother's car up to our house.

The car came, with Alan Flynn in it, and a policewoman in uniform sitting beside him.

They parked around the back, where the barn comes smack against our kitchen. That way no one entering or leaving it could be seen from the lane, or the road, or assorted hedgerows where cameramen might be hiding out.

Alan went into our house, everybody had a cup of tea, and then the car drove away again, with Alan driving and a policewoman in the front seat beside him.

This time, the policewoman was our Margaret, our personal policewoman.

Mum and Ruth were covered by a blanket

118

in the boot.

Ruth says that the drive was an awful experience. By the time they were clear of the reporters and able to stop, she had a terrible cramp. I can't imagine how they fitted into the boot of the Flynns' old car, but they did. The boot lid was open a tiny bit, tied in position with string by Alan, so that they wouldn't suffocate. Alan drove down through Cloughanny and a mile or two up the road, and then he stopped and they were able to take their places in the car.

Ruth says Alan was wonderful, but he would keep trying to talk to Mum to keep her spirits up, and he kept saying very cheerful and inappropriate things. It was grisly, but not as grisly as what was to come.

The police had set up their headquarters at the tourist viewpoint where the van had been found. They had the area taped off, but not unnaturally the Press and photographers were camped out as close to the scene of operations as they could get.

It was quite plain that Mum and Ruth couldn't go waltzing down to the waterside there, police tapes or not. So they went further along the road, to the hill head at Clonmore, and stopped the car there, on top.

Mum and Ruth got out and trudged down the fields to the lakeside, by Elmore's Rock. This would be about a mile and a quarter around the little bay at Plumber's Point. Alan Flynn wanted to go too, in case they got caught on the rusty wire by the edge of the mud, but Margaret delayed him somehow, and in the end he understood what she was at, and let them go alone.

There were four boats and divers bobbing up and down on the choppy grey water.

Ruth says it seemed all grey to her: the sky and the Silver Ridge mountains beyond and the deep dark water, that was pocked by the wind.

It was icy cold, and they stood there, for what seemed like ages, not saying anything, watching the police frogmen searching. The frogmen and the men rowing the boats were shouting to each other, and the whole of the little bay was marked out with bobbing floats, as if it were a regatta. I suppose they were sectioning it, so that they wouldn't search the same place twice, or miss me altogether.

"Suzie Q isn't in there," Mum told Ruth again.

This time, Ruth believed her. They were both up almost to their ankles in mud, but they hugged each other, and then they started back.

Ruth says that she doesn't know what convinced her, when she had set out from home so certain that I was dead. She had been trying to make herself *not* believe it, for Mum's sake, but believing it just the same. She woke up that morning with Mum already downstairs and the bed empty beside her, and she knew she couldn't go on trying to fool herself. She had to go and see for herself.

Once she was there, she says, looking at the dirty grey water and the mud and the reeds and the desolation of the place, something shifted inside her. She says the fear of what might have happened to me didn't go away from her, but somehow she knew that a watery grave at Plumber's Point wasn't part of it, and Mum had been right all along.

"You can call them off," she told the policewoman. "My sister isn't in there."

Then they drove down to the Seymour Arms at Claddagh Corner and went in for coffee and sandwiches in the lounge bar.

Alan Flynn insisted on paying, even when Margaret said it would all be on the police. Alan is very particular about his mother's money, and Mrs Flynn had given him cash to pay for anything the Quinns might need while they were in her car, so Alan insisted on paying. He is twenty-six, failed to make it to Agricultural College because he couldn't manage the exams, and lives at home on his mother's handouts and the dole. He is also one of the nicest, kindest people I know, and as honest as the day is long.

The only upsetting bit was when Willie Moore, who owns the Seymour Arms, stopped

Mum on the way out and said he was sorry for her trouble, which is the phrase people around here use when they meet someone after a bereavement.

"Suzie's alive!" Mum snapped, and she left old Willie with his face down in his boots.

"Mum's all upset, Willie," Ruth told him.

"Is the wee girl found yet?" Willie asked.

Ruth shook her head.

"They're in the wrong place," Willie told her, with true fisherman enthusiasm. "Anything that went in where your sister went in would be washed up near the overflow pipe, not around the point at all."

"My sister Suzie isn't there, Willie," Ruth told him, because by this time she says she'd become infected by Mum's certainty.

"Well, now, I hope you're right," he said, clearly disbelieving her. "But if the poor girl is in the water, that's where she'll wash up."

"Come on, Ruth," said Margaret Campbell, and she hustled Ruth out before he could say anything else, leaving him staring up at the dead fish in their glass cases behind the bar.

You would think Willie Moore would have had more sense than to talk that way to Ruth, but he didn't.

They drove home in silence.

"No doubt Willie meant well," Mum said, and that was all there was about it.

This time Mum refused to go back in the

boot, and they just drove through the line of parked cars down the side of the road opposite our place.

Ruth says Mum sat looking in front of her, never batting an eye at all the fuss that was going on. Margaret Campbell had radioed ahead, and the police had come down and started moving the Press men about and generally hassling them about being there at all. This led to a whole argument with them flashing their Press passes and demanding police co-operation with the media, all grouped around the Sergeant who was giving the orders, and that created sufficient diversion for the car to be able to get through and up the lane.

There was a photograph in the next day's editions just the same, but all it showed was two tiny figures standing in the mud. It must have been taken from somewhere up on the Silver Ridge, with a zoom lens. You couldn't make out Mum's face at all. It upset Ruth because it was an intrusion. I hope the cameraman who took it can sleep well with his conscience.

As it turned out, I had made my move by the time that picture appeared, so it didn't matter anyway.

Leo had frightened me out of my wits with his gun and the ever present possibility that he might panic and shoot me. I felt that he was only pretending to himself and the others that he was in control of the situation, but he'd lost it really. I couldn't just sit there and hope any longer; I had to escape from the hut. Getting out of it was planned already, but the bit after that had me worried.

Even if the only thing I could think of to do next was dodgy and dangerous, I had to take my chances, because nothing could be as dangerous and dodgy as just staying where I was.

It's wonderful what having no hope left does for you.

My adrenaline was running at a trot. I had to take risks, so I did, even though I knew I was gambling with my life.

CHAPTER FOURTEEN

My kidnappers were all tucked up in their sleeping bags, secure in the knowledge that I was padlocked inside a stone hut with no way out through the floor, door, walls, or non-existent windows.

They were certain that I couldn't escape, but if they had been a bit brighter, they might have stopped to think about the roof. If they had, they would have been more careful to tie me up again rather than throw me in on the floor.

An old rusty tin roof on a stone hut in an abandoned quarry – the wind and the rain had had a long time to work on it. The beams securing it, the few that still existed, were soft to the touch when I tried them. I was able to pull bits of wood off just by digging in my fingers.

Tentative shoving at the old tin established that very little force would lift the bottom edge of the roof clear of the rotten beam it was fixed to. There wouldn't be any great breaking or tearing noise if I worked loose the big nails holding the tin before raising it.

Having made the decision to spend the night in the hut and make my escape at daybreak, when at least I'd be able to see where I was going, I had plenty of time to work on the roof.

I left it till dawn. Then I took my heart in my hands and gave the roof the full works, shoving it up with all my might. I risked the squeaks, hoping they'd all be asleep.

The nails easily lifted clear of the remains of the rotten beam that ran along the top of the wall.

I got my arms through, then my head, wondering if loosening the brittle tin at the side of the hut would make the tin that was concreted into the wall of the house squeak, and give me away. It did squeak, but not very much.

Shoulders, body. I was half in and half out, pushing down on the stones to get my hips clear. The wall wasn't very high, but it was still quite a drop to the ground and I was coming out head first.

I made it, without much difficulty.

That was the easy bit, getting out of the hut. Once out, though, there was nowhere I could hide, and precious little chance of getting away on foot. I was just too far from civilization.

The next bit was supposed to be simple and straightforward: steal Gerard's bike and ride

126

my way to freedom. Probably they would hear the noise it made when it started, but even if they tried to come after me, I calculated that the bike would outspeed their old car on the rough road.

Only one problem about it. I have never ridden a motorbike. I didn't have a clue how to start the engine.

I tiptoed my way over to it.

As I'd spotted before, the keys were in the ignition ... so far so good, if what I thought was the ignition was the ignition, and not something else. Just turn the key, the engine would start, and I'd be away.

If...

Well, *if* a motorbike starts that way, like a car.

I didn't know whether bikes worked that way. I'd seen bikers, and I had a notion that they didn't just turn a key and roar off. They always seem to kick the thing your foot rests on, revving the engine loudly and twisting the handlebars. I had a notion the handlebars were some kind of throttle.

Their bikes make a lot of noise.

Once I started kicking and twisting and throttling, I was going to wake everybody up, and the bike still might not start for me.

I made myself think through that one.

Wheel the bike away from the house, for a start. Then get it to the top of a slope, because people push cars down slopes to start them and that might work for bikes as well.

That is when I found out you don't just wheel old motorbikes, you have to really push them, especially uphill over shale and rocks.

I got it to the highest point I could manage on the rough road, about thirty metres from the house, pointing downhill.

That's when I heard the yelling behind me as Gerard came out of the house. The next moment, the three of them were running towards me, shouting.

I had no time to think.

I jumped on the bike and turned the key, at the same moment shoving off with my feet, so that the bike started rolling down the slope. Then I kicked like crazy at the pedal and the thing worked.

There was a great roar out of it and it bucked like a horse. Maybe I had throttled too much, maybe the angle the bike was at affected the level of fuel in the tank in some way, but the bike didn't just start, it exploded into motion, careering down the slope toward the turn in the road, slithering and bouncing on the stones and shale.

I can't put together what happened next.

I think I must have hit one of the stones in the road, but suddenly the whole thing came apart and I was coming off the bike with my hands up to save myself as I headed for the ground, and then I was sliding and slithering on the shale, slap into a big rock. And the next thing I knew there was a huge explosion and my hair was burning and my clothes were burning and I was rolling over and over down the bank at the side of the road and I thought, *I'm dead*. By rights I should have been; I certainly could have been, but I wasn't.

I remember lying on the ground with blistering heat and roaring and banging going on all around me, and then I think I must have blacked out momentarily, just before they got to me.

I was lucky; the burning didn't amount to much more than singed eyebrows and the back of my anorak, and I don't understand that because Dodie says there was a real inferno around me from the burning fuel after the gas tank fractured. She says somehow the flame was going one way and I'd been thrown the other, so she was able to pull me away from it. The side of my face was badly lacerated from the fall and I damaged my left thumb, but otherwise I was OK. She says I was moaning and shrieking when she got to me and she thought I was badly hurt, which started her yelling at the other two for help.

Leo was almost crying. "She's wrecked Gerard's bike, the bitch. She's done the poor bastard's bike."

There were tears on his fat freckled face, the

famous face which I was seeing for the first time and which, even in my pain and wooziness, I knew I didn't know. It was really amazing. This guy runs robberies and sticks a gun in my neck and he starts to weep because his friend's motorbike is wrecked.

Gerard just stood, watching his bike burn. There was a great column of black smoke pouring up into the sky. Then Dodie panicked. She started yelling that people would see the smoke and the police would be up the mountain in no time to check it out.

"We've got to go before the cops come!" she shouted at Leo. "Get in the car now!"

That's how we ended up on our last panic-stricken journey, bumping and jolting our way along the rough road along the side of Stonecutters Mountain.

CHAPTER FIFTEEN

We drove.

Gerard was pale, chewing his lip, his precious motorbike helmet clasped on his lap, though now that the motorbike had gone that seemed sad. Dodie was driving erratically, hitting numerous potholes and skidding about the road, out of gear half the time.

I was crouched in the front passenger seat.

Leo was beside Gerard in the back of the car, playing with his gun against my neck. His hand was shaking, as if he was having some kind of trembling fit. He kept sniffing, and wiping the side of his face with his hand.

He's going to kill me was the only thought that started me talking, yet again, in the hope that I could somehow stop things from happening before everything went too far.

"What are you going to do, Leo?" I gabbled desperately, because if I was going to get through to anyone now, it had to be Leo. The time for working Dodie, or trying to soften up Gerard by offering the faint prospect of plumbing employment had long passed. Leo had the gun. It was Leo I had to placate.

"You'll never get through the roadblocks with me like this," I ploughed on. "You know that. You'll all get caught. And if you try busting through them, we'll all be shot, because the soldiers have guns and they'll think you are IRA on a job and they'll spray the car and ask questions afterwards. You should chuck me out and keep on going yourselves."

"If we hit any roadblocks, you're our ticket!" Leo said.

"You're crazy—"

"Shut up!" from Leo, and he pressed the gun against the back of my head again, patting my cheek. "No more lip out of you. And you do what you're told if we meet anybody. Right?"

There was no point in trying to argue with him. Dodie and Gerard said nothing. Dodie was red in the face and close to crying, and Gerard just sat at the back and sulked. I could see his face in the mirror. He had a gallows look on him.

Crunch-bump-crunch along the rough road, and half the time I was scared she was going to drive us right off it, over the edge of the road and down, down, down on to the rough ground below.

"Put your foot down, Dodie," Leo said.

"This isn't going to work," I said.

"I told you to shut up," he said.

I was in no position to argue. I shut up.

There would be police or army or both at any roadblock, and they would be on the lookout for us, but what could they do? Leo would show them the gun and tell them he was going to shoot me and they would have to let us through, wouldn't they?

I had no alternative but to sit there and hope that they would, because if they didn't, I might be dead. The more I thought about it, the clearer it seemed that sooner or later there would be shooting, and if there was shooting, I was the first in line for a bullet through the head.

I had to *think*.

The only other thing going for me was that as we came out of the valley, we moved into countryside that I knew. Stonecutters Mountain lies out west of Sabbath Hill, about ten miles north of Cloughanny, beyond the back of the Silver Ridge, rising above the Plantation, and now that we'd come further along the bumpy old rough road, I had at least some clue as to the lie of the land. There was a bit of comfort in that, but not a lot.

The road was winding, just a track along the side of the mountain, towards Egg Rock. I knew that there was a fork beyond Egg Rock, with one side running down to Sabbath Hill and the other going off in the direction of Balmollet, towards Quarnie Rock. The border with the Republic is that way, so I supposed they'd go left, if there was no sign of road-blocks.

So long as they were on the rough road, they were all right, because there wouldn't be road-blocks up there. I knew that. The army doesn't set up roadblocks on a road that goes to a dis-used quarry, but once we hit Sabbath Hill or the Balmollet road over the pass, we could run into one around any corner.

The rough road straggled down towards the Plantation and ran close alongside it. The road was above the top of the trees, with an almost sheer bank of rubble and broken stone falling from the side down to Warney's Stream. Dad had always meant to take Ruth and me along it, but he never did.

Bruised and battered as I was, I made up my mind that if the car stopped, I'd try to pull something and get away from them. That started me charting what I'd be up against, if I managed it.

The bank of rubble fell away to a stretch of ground that varied according to the lie of the road. Sometimes it was twenty metres from the stream, sometimes forty. It was soggy, marshy ground, with big grey rocks coming up out of it. Beyond the stream there was a broken-down barbed-wire fence about two metres high, and beyond that again the Plantation. It was a dark mass of pine trees set in regimented rows, with shadowy alleys in between, where the light was all but cut out by the foliage overhead. The ground beneath the trees was one huge cushion of brown decaying pine needles, with rocks jutting out of the middle of them.

If I was in there, dodging between the trees, he wouldn't be able to shoot me.

So, *if* the car stopped, and I got a sniff of a chance, I'd be off into the wood. Then I thought about it again, and decided that they'd never stop the car and let me out. Why should they stop at all?

I'd forgotten the obvious reason for stopping: the gate!

Even the slope of a mountain like Stonecutters belongs to someone. The rotten, lumpy grey rock-strewn ground was divided into grey rock-strewn fields, and when we came to the crossroads, there was a gate on it. No fence either side, but a gate on the road!

They must have forced the padlock on the gate to get along the rough road, but they had had the wit to close it behind them, to cover their tracks, and that meant somebody had to get out to open it, which meant they had to stop the car.

Gerard heaved himself out of the back and walked towards it.

Dodie opened her door.

"Where are you going?" from Leo.

"I'm going to speak to Gerard," she said.

"No, you're not," from Leo. "You stay where you are."

"You can't stop me."

"You stay where you are!" he repeated fiercely.

Gerard was still struggling to move the gate. It was a rotten old thing, wired up to a crumbling railway sleeper pillar, and it lay over sideways, so it took a bit of moving.

"Give us a hand, Leo!" he shouted.

"Fool!" from Leo.

He opened the door at his side, but he didn't get out.

"It needs lifting at both ends!" Gerard said, giving up.

"You make a move and I'll shoot you," Leo said to me. "That's a promise. Understand? You watch her, Dodie."

"Yes," I said.

He got out of the car and walked the fifteen metres towards Gerard.

I looked at Dodie.

She must have read what was going through my mind. She knew I'd tried to escape twice before, and that this was the third time. Dodie had only to shout out to Leo, and she could have stopped me, but she didn't. I think she didn't because she knew inside herself that it was all over, they were going to be caught, and she didn't see any sense in it.

"I've got to, Dodie," I said.

Leo got to the gate, as my hand went towards the door handle.

"No!" she whispered. "No, don't, Suzie!"

They were both struggling with the gate and it was the only chance I was going to get.

"No, Suzie!" but her voice was still low, directed at me only, so they couldn't hear.

Go-go-go!

I was out of the door, sprawling momentarily on the side of the bank, then I threw myself on in a half run, half stagger, down, down, down over the stones, my feet slipping and sliding on the mud and heather.

"NO, SUZIE!" Dodie shrieked at me from the car.

CHAPTER SIXTEEN

I landed at the bottom of the slope and then I was up and running. I heard Leo and Gerard shouting behind me, but I don't know what they shouted. I put down my head and plunged on towards the Plantation fence, willing myself not to look back.

Then my feet went from under me and I was slipping and sliding, and I crashed right into the stream, sprawling in the water.

Gerard was on the road above me, yelling. Then he took off in a great leap, heading for me.

I was up out of the water and scrambling to get over the barbed wire that lay between me and the trees. Then my sweater snagged on the wire and I was struggling to free it.

Gerard was on his hands and knees where he'd lost his footing. He came up and launched himself down the slope towards me, just as I ripped clear of the wire and got under the trees.

Bang.

Leo fired his gun.

Whizz-bang-whizz-bang. A bullet ricocheting off the rocks.

And a yelp, behind me.

I've never been shot at before. I was thinking, *Don't shoot me, don't shoot me.*

I don't think Leo meant to shoot me. I hope the shots were fired to make me realize that he could, and he would shoot, if he had to – that I had to stop. I think it was a split-second reaction on his part, when he saw me running away. Maybe he fired towards the ground and the noises I heard were the ricochets of the bullets coming off a rock. Either that or Gerard ran blindly across his line of fire, concentrating on getting to me.

The next thing I heard was somebody screaming. It was Dodie.

I turned.

Gerard was down on his haunches, half kneeling. He fell over on his side, and lay there.

Nobody moved.

Dodie was by the car, her hands up at her head, as if she was trying to stop it from bursting. Leo was about fifteen metres away from her, by the open gate, standing, looking stunned with the gun in his hand. I was in the trees, my feet sunk deep in the damp pine needles.

Nothing happened. We just stood there, all of us looking at Gerard. I don't know how long we stayed frozen.

Gerard turned his head, and his back arched for a moment, and then a whole flow of blood came out of his mouth and down over his chest.

It can't be happening. It can't be happening, was running through my head. But it was. It had happened.

I remember realizing how cold it was suddenly, and how the damp of the pine needles was leaking into my trainers, and how I would need a change of socks.

Dodie was the first to move.

"Oh my God! Oh God!" Dodie shouted, and she came skidding down the bank at the side of the road, scrabbling her way towards Gerard.

She lay down on top of him, cradling his head, and there was blood all down her red shirt.

"Help me! Help me!" she cried.

Leo moved slowly, as if he were in a dream. Gerard's friend, his big mate, who had just shot him, walked towards the car with a dazed look on his face.

He got into the car and sat there in the driver's seat, with his head down.

"Help me! Help me!" moaned Dodie. "Somebody help me!"

I couldn't leave her like that. I had to go back, however much I was afraid of Leo.

As I reached her, I heard the car engine start.

"Leo! Leo!" Dodie screamed, ignoring me.

The car moved slowly, bumping and grating

on the rough stone road.

"Leo!" Dodie called.

Then I was down on the ground beside her, trying to hold her. Dodie was quaking and shivering and stroking her Gerard, and trying to mop up the blood with her sleeve.

"Help me. Help me."

Again and again and again.

"Help me. Help me. Help me."

There was nothing I could do to help her.

The worst of it all was when we had to leave him there. She didn't want to. She didn't want him to be cold. We put my sweater over him and then I told her that we had to go, that he would want us to go. I said something about the baby and how there would be something for her that was his and she had to be sure she didn't harm the baby, that was why we had to go, and why we had to leave him.

I don't know what words I used. The words didn't matter really.

The best thing I could do was hug her and hold her and try to start her moving.

It was a long way down, stumbling along the track between the grey boulder walls, with the mountainside gaunt and rough on either side of us, and no one to see us but a few sheep. I was part carrying her and part hugging her. Her face was set as if she were going to cry inside forever.

That walk, clinging on to Dodie, half carrying her some of the time, seemed to last an eternity.

She started mumbling and crying that Gerard was alone and she couldn't leave him. Twice she tried to go back, because Gerard was alone and she couldn't leave Gerard alone and poor Gerard would be cold. I almost had to drag her down the road.

I said something about the baby, and she screamed at me, just once, her voice echoing at me off the granite boulder walls on either side of the road. Then it was back to walking.

In the end she followed me, two or three steps behind, all the way back to the world, which turned out to be a Mrs McKibben's house. She had no telephone and no car, but she sent her husband Billy down on the bike to the next house, and the people there telephoned for the police and an ambulance.

Dodie and I sat in Mrs McKibben's front room watching *Neighbours* on TV, waiting for them to come for us. We were surrounded by the icons of her life: pictures of her son and his wife and family. She told us they were in Boston and he was driving a taxi and the kids were doing great at school, and her daughter-in-law was taking night classes in computer technology and business management. He was a great son to her, only he didn't manage to get home often enough because living is very expensive in Boston.

She wanted Mr McKibben to take her out

there on a visit, and they were saving up the money and maybe they would get across to see her sister Ethel in Florida, but then maybe they wouldn't be able to. Her sister Ethel had married a GI who was stationed over here in the War, and they had a big house and a swimming pool that they shared with the people in the place next door.

It all seemed happy and comfortable and unreal to me, and I suppose the same was true for Dodie. It didn't seem to connect up at all with what we'd just been through.

Then Mum and Ruth came with the police – our policewoman Margaret as it happens, although I didn't know her then as well as I do now.

And Mum was on Mrs McKibben's sofa hugging me, and she was crying and I was crying and Ruth was crying.

"You really did it this time, Suzie Q!" Ruth said.

And somehow that started us laughing and there was this wild three-way laugh and hug going on, with us all rolling about on the sofa.

Dodie was sitting slumped in the armchair by the door, watching us, looking like a dead person propped up on Mrs McKibben's fussy little cushions.

I can still see her pale face and her big expressionless eyes, with the rims red from crying.

CHAPTER SEVENTEEN

It should never have happened. That's really all I can say – although anyone can say that and it doesn't mean much.

It is what keeps running through my head, though. It should never have happened to Mum and me in the supermarket. Little Davie should never have had his birthday messed up the way it was. It should never have happened to Danny Semple or his daughter May, or Ruth, or Alan Flynn down the lane with his mum, but we were all caught up in it. It was their fault, Dodie and her Gerard and Leo.

So how come I end up feeling guilty, especially about little Dodie and her baby?

We're liberal thinkers, the Quinns, by Irish standards anyway. That means we've taken onboard all there is to know about poverty and delinquency and teenage pregnancies, which is true. It is also true that Dodie and Leo and Gerard did what they did for their own selfish reasons. We were their victims, not the other way about. That's not to deny all the harsh background information about their lives. I know all that. I can understand why they felt desperate enough to do what they did, but understanding is as far as I can take it. What they did was wrong and I don't think anyone should try to excuse it.

To be fair, Dodie didn't try to make excuses.

I went to see her with Ruth, after the court case – she asked me to, not the other way around.

Most of what she had to say was about Gerard, trying to make out that what happened wasn't his fault, and by extension it wasn't supposed to be Leo's either. In Dodie's version, a lot of it was *her* fault. She wouldn't even tell the police who the woman was who had helped them, the woman whose house I couldn't find, whose voice I couldn't recognize. Maybe it was misguided loyalty on Dodie's part, but I think it was more that she held herself to blame; if it hadn't been for the unplanned pregnancy, none of it would have happened. She would have lived happy ever after with her Gerard. In a perverse way, she felt she killed her boyfriend ... well, *husband* really...

"That's daft, Dodie," I told her. "It's Leo who ruined your life. Saying you're to blame for all that happened makes no sense at all."

Long face from Dodie, clearly disagreeing.

"I don't think Dodie's life is ruined," Ruth said, suddenly very practical. "Why should it be? You seem a very strong person to me, Dodie, and you'll have your baby to care for. You'll come through."

"Yeh. I will, won't I?" Dodie said.

I did what I could to help her at the trial.

I laid it on thick with the police about how good she had been, how she had helped me and nursed me and brought me food and even loosened my bonds for me. I tried to imply that she'd been dragged along by the other two, that all along she had been a victim of big bad Leo and her weak-kneed Gerard.

It helped a bit, Mum says. But it was all such a mess anyway that nothing could help very much. One little robbery gone wrong and look at the lives that were smashed.

Dorothy Michelle Rice, aged sixteen, unemployed, wound up having her baby in a Supervised Centre for Convicted Persons, down near Lurgan. She sent me a card with lilacs on it, announcing the arrival of Gerard James Rice, six pounds, two ounces. I sent her a little blue jumpsuit with a rabbit on it. I suppose babies are allowed their own clothes in a place like that, even if the mothers aren't. Maybe they are. I never went to see her baby. I don't like to think about what will happen to little Gerard James Rice when he grows up.

146

Gerard Michael Rice, aged seventeen, apprentice plumber, unemployed, was dead. Gerard's mum came to see me before the trial. She wanted to clear her Gerard's name, because he was dead and couldn't defend himself. She'd picked up Dodie's own line: it was all that girl's fault for leading her good boy on and getting herself pregnant so that Gerard would have to marry her. Mum threatened her with the police for trying to intimidate a witness.

Leo Arthur William Seymour, aged nineteen, labourer, unemployed, was picked up trying to siphon petrol from the back of a truck parked outside a pub somewhere near Dundalk. How Leo made it over the border, past checkpoints, in the state he was in I don't know. He threw the gun in the canal at Newry. He had once worked with a repair team who dug up the road outside our house, which is why he thought I would recognize him. Leo went to prison, which serves him right for all the pain he caused me and my mum and Ruth.

Alan Flynn, aged twenty-six, unemployed, from the end of our lane, was bound over to keep the peace for discharging a shotgun in a manner likely to cause injury or destruction to property: in this case shooting out windscreens.

Last but not least, the World Famous Suzie Q, aged fifteen, is back at school studying. Mum and Ruth and my teachers are all being very supportive. I have some marks on my legs that the doctors say will disappear over the years. They also tell me that the scars on the side of my face will one day look like extra laugh lines. They certainly don't look like laugh lines now, and I can't see how they ever will, but that is what happens if you go around falling off motorbikes and letting them explode on you. The thumb mended just fine.

It should be Happy Ever After Time at the Quinns' house, I suppose, but life isn't as easy as that. I keep seeing Dodie propped up on the fancy cushions in Mrs McKibben's front room.

I'll never forget the dead look on her face.

TANGO'S BABY
by Martin Waddell

Brian Tangello – Tango – is not one of life's romantic heroes. Even his few friends are amazed to learn of his love affair with young Crystal O'Leary, the girl he fancies and who seemed to have no interest in him. Next thing they know, she's pregnant – and that's when the real story of Tango's baby begins. By turns tragic and farcical, it's a story in which many claim a part, but few are able to help Tango as he strives desperately to keep his new family together.

"Stylishly written, sensitive, funny and moving… A book with a depth that can only reward all who read it." *The Times*

"Waddell is as ever an excellent storyteller." *The Independent*

"Brilliantly written." *The Sunday Telegraph*

THE LIFE AND LOVES
OF ZOË T. CURLEY
by Martin Waddell

It's not easy being an aspiring teenager with a brace and the body of a "fat elephant".

This is the lot of Zoë T. Curley, prisoner of Zog, the life-system invented by Zoë's temperamental writer father to keep order in the Curley household. Fortunately Zoë has a loyal best friend, Melissa, with whom she can discuss her many domestic woes, as well as such vital matters as BOYS and LOVE. Follow Zoë's fluctuating fortunes throughout one turbulent month in this entertaining diary novel.

"Acutely observed." *The Daily Mail*

TRAVELLING HOPEFULLY
by Judy Allen

When her mother is taken into hospital, thirteen-year-old Clare finds herself accompanying Maggie, her journalist aunt, on a whistlestop tour of Devon to research a series of magazine articles. The two are unlikely and – at least initially – antagonistic travelling companions. Sparks fly on the flints of their mutually sharp wit. But, by the end of their travels, will they arrive at some kind of understanding?

Whitbread Award winner Judy Allen tells a lively, humorous and explosive story.

"Crisp dialogue and a refreshingly original use of words amuse and divert... Absorbing reading." *The Guardian*

BADGER ON THE BARGE
by Janni Howker

"This set of five stories, each concerned with a relationship between young and old, is quality stuff... Not to be missed."
The Times Educational Supplement

These fine stories abound with absorbing situations and memorable characters. Meet cussed, rebellious Miss Brady, who lives with a badger on a barge; the reviled old shepherd Reicker; Sally Beck, topiary gardener with an extraordinary past; the reclusive Egg Man; proudly independent Jakey ... and the young people whose lives they profoundly affect.

Winner of the International Reading Association Children's Book Award. Shortlisted for the Whitbread Children's Novel Award and the Carnegie Medal.

SO MUCH TO TELL YOU
by John Marsden

Scarred, literally, by her past, Marina has withdrawn into silence.

She speaks to no one. But, set the task of writing a diary by her English teacher, she finds a way of expressing her thoughts and feelings and of exploring the traumatic events that have caused her distress. There is so much she has to say...

"Beautifully written... The heroine's perceptiveness, sense of humour and fairmindedness temper the tragedy and offer a splendid read."
The Times Educational Supplement

"A moving chronicle of personal recovery."
The Observer

THE BOY OF MY DREAMS
by Dyan Sheldon

When will she meet him, the guy, the one, the boy of her dreams? When will she fall in love?

Michelle, commonly known as Mike, just can't stop thinking about it. And then it happens. She meets Him. Bill. He's gorgeous. He's cool. He's in college. Mike thinks Bill is her destiny. Bill says they look good together. But Bone, Mike's oldest friend, thinks her hormones are damaging her brain...

This rib-tickling, heart-wrenching tale, by the author of *Tall, Thin and Blonde*, depicts a pivotal moment in one girl's life, as she searches for love – and discovers herself!

TO TRUST A SOLDIER
by Nick Warburton

"The rules of war, Mary. You must promise to keep them or it might be the death of us all."

Sometime in a machine-less future, six soldiers – five volunteers and a professional – are on their way to fight for their country against an invading army, when they come across a teenage girl, Mary. She becomes their map, guiding them to the battlefield – or so the men are told by their leader, the flinty, dispassionate Sergeant Talbot, whom they trust as deeply as they distrust Mary. One though, young Hobbs, feels sorry for the girl and a relationship develops between them…

"Warburton has a remarkable gift for realistic writing." *The Times*

THE TIME TREE
by Enid Richemont

The tall tree in the park is Rachel and Joanna's special place.

It's Anne's too. So it hardly seems surprising that the three girls meet up there – except for the fact that Anne was born over four hundred years ago!

"A very unusual ghost story." *Books*

"An enchanting and imaginative story, which will give modern children an idea of how it must have felt to be a child in the Elizabethan age." *The Lady*

DOUBLE VISION
by Diana Hendry

"People would do a lot better if they could see double like me... I mean seeing things two ways – with the head and the heart."

Growing up in a small, North West coastal town in the 1950s, fifteen-year-old Eliza Bishop finds life unbearably claustrophobic. But to her small, fearful sister Lily, the seaside setting affords unlimited scope for her imagination. Through these two very different pairs of eyes a memorable range of characters, events and emotions is brought clearly into vision.

"Succeeds totally where very few books do, as a novel which bestrides the two worlds of adult and children's fiction with total success in both... The stuff of which the very best fiction is wrought." *The Sunday Times*

THE FLOWER KING
by Lesley Howarth

The narrator of this story doesn't just see colours, he *feels* them. At home, the colour is mainly panic-button red. But on Saturdays, visiting old Mrs Pinder, a hopeful yellow floods in. It's the yellow of the daffodil fields where "Pinny" worked as a child for William Bowhays Johns, the Flower King, whose tragic story lies at the heart of this absorbing tale.

Shortlisted for the Whitbread Children's Novel Award and the Guardian Children's Fiction Award.

"Characterization is deft, the descriptive passages lyrical, the dialogue tone perfect."
Michael Morpurgo, The Guardian

"A pleasure ... assured and original."
Gillian Cross, The Times Educational Supplement (Books of the Year)

MORE WALKER PAPERBACKS
For You to Enjoy